SUGAR

SUGAR

Jewell Parker Rhodes

LITTLE, BROWN AND COMPANY
New York   Boston

Little, Brown and Company

Hachette Book Group
237 Park Avenue, New York, NY 10017
Visit our website at lb-kids.com

Little, Brown and Company is a division of Hachette Book Group, Inc.
The Little, Brown name and logo are trademarks of Hachette Book Group, Inc.

The publisher is not responsible for websites (or their content) that are not owned by the publisher.

First Paperback Edition: June 2014
First published in hardcover in May 2013 by Little, Brown and Company

Library of Congress Cataloging-in-Publication Data

Rhodes, Jewell Parker.
    Sugar / Jewell Parker Rhodes.—1st ed.
       p. cm.
    Summary: In 1870, Reconstruction brings big changes to the Louisiana sugar plantation where spunky ten-year-old Sugar has always lived, including her friendship with Billy, the son of her former master, and the arrival of workmen from China.
    ISBN 978-0-316-04305-2 (hc)—ISBN 978-0-316-04306-9 (pb)
    [1. Plantation life—Louisiana—Fiction.   2. Race relations—Fiction.   3. African Americans—Fiction.   4. Chinese Americans—Fiction.   5. Reconstruction (U.S. history, 1865–1877)—Fiction.   6. Louisiana—History—1865–1950—Fiction.]   I. Title.
    PZ7.R3476235Sug 2013
    [Fic]—dc23

                                                                                        2012026218

10 9 8 7 6 5 4 3 2 1

RRD-C

Printed in the United States of America

Book design by Alison Impey

Love and thanks to
Edwardo Lao Rhodes,
who inspired the novel, and
to Adam Ryan Livingston,
who inspired Billy.

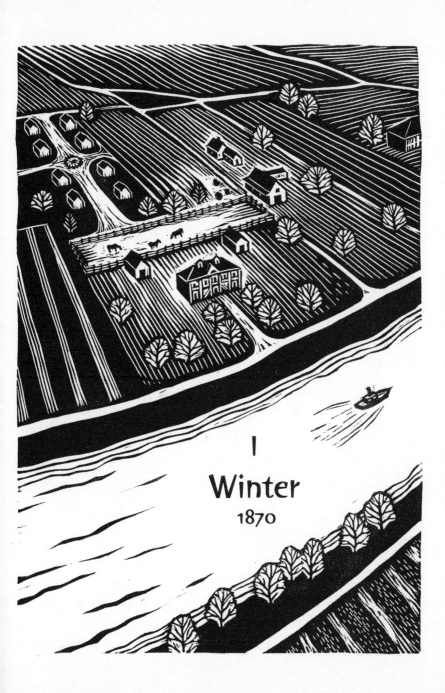

I

Winter

1870

River Road Plantation

Everybody likes sugar.

Folks say, "There wouldn't be any good food without sugar." Like rhubarb cobbler. Blueberry pie. Yellow cake.

But I hate sugar. I won't eat it. Not ever.

"No sweets, just savories," I used to tell Ma. "Corn bread. Grits." Even nasty okra and green beans are better than sugar.

There's all kinds of sugar. Crystals that turn lemons into lemonade. Syrup that cools into taffy. Or pralines, brittle. There's even sugarcane you can suck until your lips wrinkle and pucker.

In the mill, there're mountains of sugar ready to be shipped from Louisiana to the whole wide world.

Ma would say, "Most folks think sugar is something in a tin cup or a china bowl. They don't know sugar is hard."

"Hard," I'd echo as she poured well water into a bowl.

"Months of planting, hoeing, harvesting. Bones aching, sweat stinging your eyes. Dirt clings everywhere."

"Beneath nails, toes. Even in my hair," I'd complain before splashing my face with water.

Me and Ma always smelled of sugar, sweat, and dirt.

"What did I smell like when I was born?"

"Spring," she'd whisper, wiping my face dry. "Not Planting-Day spring. Just spring. Blooming, lemony, and fresh."

I wish I could remember that clean smell.

When I was two days old, Ma strapped me to her back and cut cane.

Nights, we ate cornmeal cakes. Then me and Ma would lie on our hay mattress on the packed-dirt floor.

"Sugar's hard," she'd sigh, kissing my cheek, twice, before sleep.

Before another day tending cane.

ॐ

River Road is almost nothing but cane. There're two rows of slave shacks. Mostly empty now. There's the big plantation house where the Willses live. The mill where cane is boiled and dried into crystals. The stable and henhouse.

The rest is cane. Growing ten feet high, row after row, as far as the eye can see. When wind blows, cane hisses, comes alive, swaying like a dancing forest. Thin, pointy leaves lick the air, flapping like streamers. It's pretty. 'Til you get close. Then sugar gets nastier than any gator.

Sugar bites a hundred times, breaking skin and making you bleed. Each leaf has baby teeth on all its edges. Even with work gloves, tiny red pricks itch everywhere. My cheeks get smacked. By harvest's end, my face, hands, and arms are all cut up.

Outside River Road Plantation, nobody cares who cuts cane. Nobody cares my hand swings the machete, bundles, drags stalks onto the cart.

At River Road, my hands are the youngest. Everyone else's hands, except Lizzie's (she's two years older than me), are old and wrinkled. Grown hands, stiff and scarred. Sometimes the old folks put their hands in warm water with peppermint to heal. Or rub them with fatback sprinkled with cayenne.

I've lived at River Road my entire life. Cane is all I know. Cutting, cracking, carrying pieces of cane. My back hurts. Feet hurt. Hands get syrupy. Bugs come. Sugar calls—all kinds of bugs, crawling, inching, flying. Nasty, icky bugs.

I hate, hate, hate sugar.

During harvest, Mister Wills sets lamps so folks can cut cane all night. "Cane won't wait," he says. He shouts, "Cane time, cuttin' time." Or he snarls, "Two bits extra for the most cane cut." Then, everybody speeds up and there're more tiny bites. Just like teeth chew rows of corn, sugar-teeth chew on you.

Mister Wills keeps complaining, "Not enough cane workers."

I think, *Why isn't he helping, then?*

Mister Wills just walks and watches everyone work. Behind him, Tom, the Overseer, cracks the whip, spraying dirt.

Since Emancipation, there're not enough workers. Almost everyone young enough, without gnarled, crinkly brown hands, has gone north.

"Some folks are scared to leave," said Ma. "They say, 'The bad I know is better than the bad I don't.'

They don't believe they have strength left for adventure."

"We're ready for adventure. We're strong."

"That's right," said Ma, hugging me close.

We waited for Pa, who was sold right after I was born, to come back for us. We were going to run away. Head north. We waited and waited. When the war started, Ma whispered, "Pa's fighting for the Union. I just know it. Helping to free us." We waited for him, proud, hoping. The war ended. President Lincoln won. Still, we waited. Five years of freedom and Pa still didn't come.

Then Ma got sick and died. Her strength drained like water.

I'm ten now.

I'm not a slave anymore.

I'm free.

Except from sugar.

Harvest Is Done

Tonight, folks are smiling, rocking, clapping hands. Everyone is happy, rich. Mister Wills has paid us our dollars.

Dollars won't last long. After we buy cloth, seeds, lamp oil, and chicken feed, we'll be just as poor as when we were slaves. But tonight, everyone is proud. Tonight is like Christmas.

Tomorrow, everybody can rest.

"Thank the Lord," says Mister Petey in his gravelly voice. "Another harvest done. Thank goodness, I can sleep."

I think, *Thank goodness, I can play. Go where I want. Do what I want.*

"No need to wake early," says Missus Ellie, tired, her chin quivering. Sick or well, she cuts cane. Like me, she has no blood family. "I'll sleep 'til noon."

I'll be up at sunrise.

The campfire crackles. Everybody's outside our stuffy shacks.

Stars are blinking. A breeze carries wet air from the Mississippi.

"No work tomorrow!" shouts Mister Beale, stretching his fingers toward the moon. All along his arms are scars, thick and knotted.

He smiles at me.

I smile back. I love Mister Beale. He tells me stories even though Missus Beale thinks they're useless. "You could be working, eating, sleeping. *Humph, humph, humph,*" she says, disapproving. "Made-up stories are a waste of good time."

I'm hoping Mister Beale will tell one of his Br'er Rabbit and Hyena tales. Tell how Rabbit tricked Hyena into falling in the river, how Hyena got stuck

on a mountain ledge. How Rabbit always fools mean
Hyena.

My eyes are heavy. Last day of harvest is as hard
as the first.

Lizzie sits down beside me, tugging her shift over
her knees, her hands folded primly in her lap.

"Hey," I say.

"Hey," she answers, her mouth downturned. Since
the Johnsons and their boys, Mo, Charlie, and Lloyd,
went north, she's been lovesick. Lizzie's stuck on
Mo, even though he's got big ears, big teeth.

Lizzie's my only friend. When we aren't working,
we've always had fun together. We're the only kids
left. But Lizzie doesn't climb trees anymore (she
sighs instead), she doesn't run (she swishes), and she
doesn't like pranks ("Childish," she says).

"Let's play rope," I say. "Tomorrow. Early, first
light."

"No."

"Next day?"

"We'll see."

Looking right, I can see the horizon, a red glow for miles in the darkness where the sugarcane used to be. I can even see clear to the big house, its windows glowing. Mister and Missus Wills are having a party, too. Manon and Annie, the house servants, roasted a pig.

I twirl my pigtail around my finger, scratch the scab on my knee.

Mister Waters, the boiler man, plays a banjo made of wood and wires. One side of his face and arm are burnt pinkish-white. Syrup, in the cauldron, bubbled and burst. His arm saved half his face. He plucks, delicate. Still, the sound is harsh and sweet, clanky and bright at the same time.

I'm still hoping for a story.

Old folks are dancing. Mister Beale stomps his feet. Missus Beale claps. Mister Petey pounds his thighs like a drum. Missus Celeste, whose job it is to watch the syrup cool and carefully separate brown crystals from white, is stepping side to side, twirling with an imaginary friend.

I glance sideways at Lizzie. She's staring at nothing, yet her face is marked with longing. My friend has disappeared. Grown up. Gotten old, older than me.

Folks who left River Road hooted and hollered: "Going north"; "Going to live up north"; "There's new life in the North." Even Mister Beale's pretty daughter and eldest son got starry-eyed and caught north fever. They begged their parents to go with them. Mister Beale told them, "We're too old, too slow."

I'm not too old or slow! But no one left will take me.

Up north, I could find new friends. Or old ones—Winnie, Charlie, and Ulysses. But I'm afraid to go by myself. No one who went north has ever come back.

Still, it's a good night. My stomach is filled with red beans, a little pork.

Tomorrow, I'll search for an eagle's nest.

I smile, then quickly squeeze my lips shut. Missus Thornton is bearing down on me. I scramble up. Just 'cause she's the preacher's wife, she feels a "calling," as Ma said, "to fix everything. And everyone!" She's got her determined "pity-pity" look. Pity poor me, she thinks. Pa gone. Ma gone. "Scrawny. Pitiful child," she says. "This is what you need."

I try to scramble away. She catches my sleeve and pushes a plate in front of my face. Bars caked with sugar. Squares of sickly sweet stuff.

I gag. I can't help it. I cover my mouth. Then drop my hands. I throw up.

Missus Thornton screams, "Sugar!"

Then I start to cry. Sugar is my name.

Freedom

I stretch, wriggling my toes, arching my back. No cane today!

Even though it's cold, I don't care. I throw off my blanket and slip on my shoes. The soles are thin; I feel every pebble. I get my shawl, wrapping it over my head and shoulders. I grab a biscuit, then dash onto the porch, wanting to crow, like Rooster Ugly, at the brightening sky. Everyone else is still asleep. Sleeping on the floor of our old slave shacks. Even Rooster Ugly hasn't stirred.

Puffs of white clouds float like meal cakes. Frost covers the dirt yard, the shacks' porches and steps.

I'm off, running. Free. Sprinting to the river, my soles flapping against my bare feet.

I run, swallowing big gulps of air. I run past cane fields, then up the grassy knoll where the big house sits to keep dry when the river overflows.

I smell the Mississippi before I see it. Muddy and tangy from algae, marsh grasses, and sedge. Nothing like sugar!

I whoop down the riverbank, kicking up dust, tiny rocks. I startle a raccoon. I pass trees, some dark and shriveled, some bright and evergreen. The sun rises, making the frost sparkle.

I see it—the Mississippi River, powerful, wide, and stretching long. Looking left or right, you can't tell where water ends.

I wave at the sailor atop a barge. He waves back.

"Take it away," I shout. "Take the sugar away!"

The sailor salutes me.

I twirl, pinch my shift, and curtsy.

Dozens of men are hauling sugar onto the barge. There are tracks that run the miles of fields, straight to the mill. From the mill, huge metal buckets of brown sugar are pushed, pulled down the tracks. Straight to the dock.

I run, fast and hard along the riverbank. Darting northward, I'm a ship chugging to St. Louis. Then I turn around and run south. *Chug-chug-chugging* down to New Orleans.

The barge hoots long and low. *Ooooo. Ooooo.*

Bye, sugar. Bye. Good riddance.

River water stretches into land, making shallow coves, streams, and swamp marshes. Dropping my shawl, I squat where the water's not too deep.

I splash my hands in the water. It's muddy brown. Reeds, grass, and algae choke the water. Bluegills skim the surface, puckering their mouths, eating bugs. A pelican dives for breakfast.

I see a turtle.

I slip off my shoes and step into the cold water. I

clench my chattering teeth. "Luck, luck, luck," Ma told me. "Touching a turtle's back brings luck."

Sand and mud are racing over my feet, through my toes. The turtle's little legs are flapping, stroking faster than I can walk. Water swirls around my knees. I take wider, bigger steps. I reach.... I reach.... I fall.

Splash.

The turtle shoots away, dives, and disappears.

I'm wet, shivering.

Quick, I stand, happy the water isn't deep. Happy there aren't any snakes. Or worse, gators.

Onshore, I squeeze water from my shift's hem.

I hear a whistle, sharp and shrill.

I stare into the trees. Wind's rustling leaves, holly bushes. Everything else is still. Quiet.

Who's out there? Overseer Tom? A chicken thief? A peddler?

I'm not afraid of them.

Chin up, I gather twigs, sticks, and dry grass. I start a small fire and sit, wrapping my shawl close. I get warm, warmer.

*　　*　　*

I undo my kerchief and bite into the biscuit.

I hear a whistle again.

Billy Wills, the owner's son, steps out of the bush. Leaves are pasted on his clothes; his face is brushed with mud.

"You've been following me?" I shout, angry. "Watching me, Billy Wills?"

Billy grins, his eyes blue as robin's eggs. "Did you guess? Did you know it was me?"

"'Course I did," I say, grumbling. But I didn't. I've always been told to keep away from Billy.

Billy stoops, palms stretched toward my fire. I'm not used to seeing him up close. His pants are wool; he has thick-soled shoes. His legs and feet aren't cold like mine. He never has to work.

"I found rabbit holes."

I don't say anything.

"They were so deep. Wide enough I could fit my arm in them. I tried to catch a rabbit, but I couldn't."

"Silly. Rabbits are smart. They saw you coming. Hyenas are dumb."

"What's a hyena?"

Mister Beale says a hyena is like a fox, but it lives in Africa. I don't tell Billy. I should go. I'm not supposed to talk to him.

Billy shouts, "Look." He jumps up, stands, upside down, on his hands.

"That's nothing." I bend, roll over twice, and leap like a rabbit.

"I can do this." Billy turns sideways, hops, then he's upside down, his feet, his hands, his whole body spinning like a wheel.

"Teach me," I shout.

"Won't."

"You're mean."

"Tell me, then—what's a hyena?"

Stubborn, I yell, "Won't."

"Sugar. Sugar. Sugar," Billy taunts.

My hands cover my ears.

"Sugar. Sugar. Sugar."

"Stop it," I scream. I will not cry. I will not!

"I'm sorry," says Billy. "I know you hate your name."

"How'd you know?"

"I hear stories from the cooks. Manon and Annie."

"Good ones?"

"Not about you."

Indignant, I roll my eyes. Grown-ups think I'm trouble.

I look at Billy. He's a mess. Like me.

I'm wet, hair tangled, with algae sticking to my feet. Billy's clay-streaked face is cracking, his hair's limp, and his twig-crown is busted into a dozen pieces on the ground.

I point at Billy, he points at me, and we both start laughing.

"Sug—" He stops, then starts again. "You made a good fire."

I smile.

"Want to play?" Billy asks.

"I thought you didn't like girls."

"Girls are okay. Pa doesn't want me to play with slaves."

"I'm not a slave. I'm free."

"Only 'cause Lincoln won. Pa says, 'Times are changing.' He doesn't like it."

21

"Do you like it, Billy Wills?"

Billy stares at the ground like there's money covering it.

I kick dirt into the fire. Sparks fly.

"I like you," he mumbles.

I don't believe my ears. Billy's face is red.

"You used to wear a yellow ribbon."

I touch my pigtail. Ma gave me that ribbon. I put it in her coffin.

"Look. Look what I got." Billy's palm opens. In his hand is a tube, woven red and yellow.

"Can I?"

Billy nods.

I pick up the tube, as long as my hand, and look through it like a telescope. I see Billy's grin.

"Isn't it pretty?"

I roll it over and over. I've never seen such a thing. It's beautiful.

"Where'd you get it?"

"Pa. He brought it from New Orleans. Try it. Put it on your fingers."

"Can I?"

"Sure."

I put one index finger in one hole, then the other finger in the second hole. The tube sparkles, bridging my two fingers and hands.

I pull my fingers outward. They're stuck!

Billy is laughing, whooping, hopping from foot to foot. "Got you. Got you."

"You tricked me." I'm madder than a bee.

"Gets them every time! You should've seen my ma, twisting. My tutor turned purple!"

"Aw," I howl. My fingers are trapped. I'm pulling, hard, my fingers are red, straining. I can't use my hands. Or even wiggle my fingers. Then, I flap my arms, high and low, like a mixed-up bird. "Take it off. Take it off."

I'm wriggling, fighting like a catfish on a line.

Billy touches my arm. "Relax." His voice is soft.

He taps the tube, so hard and bright.

"Don't pull," he says. "Push."

I push my fingers, and, magically, they're free; the tube slips off, falling into Billy's hand.

"What's it called?"

"China finger trap. Pa thought I'd like it."

"Do you?"

"Yeah. 'Specially with grown-ups. Boy, do they get mad!" He tosses the tube into the air.

I wish I had one.

"I was only playing," says Billy. "If I wasn't, I would've let you squirm all day."

Billy's not much older than me. But this is the first time we've played together. Mainly, I work. Billy's tutor makes him read books. Sometimes, he practices a violin with the windows open and it sounds like a screaming cat.

"I knew you were playing." I say, smiling. "Want to touch a turtle? They're good luck!"

৩৭

Me and Billy walk side by side. We're both soaking wet and happy. It's two miles back to River Road. Me, to my gray shack; Billy, to his yellow plantation home.

"You shouldn't come near the house. We're not supposed to be together." Billy ducks his head. Mud

24

has rinsed off his face. His cheeks are puffy white like a cloud.

Billy must be as lonely as me. Anthony, his older brother, was sent to a New Orleans school. One day Anthony was there, then gone—like Ma was there, then gone. Except Ma is never coming back.

"Is it true you don't sleep on the floor?"

"I've got a bed and pillows and blankets."

"What's a pillow?"

"A cushion for your head. Don't you know anything?"

"I know plenty," I say, but I'm thinking, *What do you need a head cushion for?*

All I've known is my bed sack filled with hay.

I hug my shawl closer. I've known Billy all my life, but I don't really *know* him.

"Each to his own place," Mister Wills says. "God didn't intend for races to mix."

"You're free now, Sugar," Ma would say, but warned, "Stay away from the big house. Trouble follows where you're not wanted. And black folks are never wanted."

*   *   *

Over my shoulder, I look at the sun setting. It looks as if it's floating on the river. I'm glad Billy followed me.

Billy's hands are stuffed in his pockets. Freckles run from his nose to his ears.

He starts whistling. I whistle, too. But I'm not as good at it as him. My whistle cracks, loses air. I wait for Billy to say something mean, but he doesn't. He just says, "Try again."

I do. My whistle trills high.

We make music all the way home.

"Night," Billy says. We squat, surrounded by bushes. Both of us don't want to leave. He's twirling the magic tube, and I'm watching the colors blur.

"Night." He moves toward the big house.

I stay low, hiding. Candles flicker in windows. There's dozens of them. I smell meat. My stomach rumbles.

Billy stops. He turns, runs back, a swaying shadow, and stoops, whispering hurriedly, "I have a secret—you can't tell. Pa says he's sending for Chinamen."

My brow wrinkles.

"They might be on the ocean now." Then Billy dashes toward the house, leaps up the porch steps, and disappears through a door bigger than any man.

I'm shivering, trembling again. I don't know what *Chinamen* means.

I'm scared. Billy has told me a secret.

Secrets are bad.

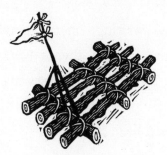

Pirate Captains

Me and Billy run off, adventuring four days in a row. I don't care if we're not supposed to! We pick wild chicory leaves; dig river holes, filling them with twigs; fish with balls of cornmeal (we don't catch nothin'); and try to trap a skunk. Grits for bait doesn't work.

We're happy.

Missus Beale isn't happy.

Every day at dusk, I try to sneak home. Missus

Beale is always waiting, on the porch, frowning, hollering at me, "Sugar, there's work to do. Off-season's short. Have you started sewing your shift?"

"No, ma'am."

"Where've you been all day?"

"Outside."

"I know outside," she says, exasperated. "But where? Doing what?"

I squirm, wiggle my toes. Ma taught me not to lie. But Missus Beale would be mad if I told the truth.

"You're not getting into trouble? Acting foolish?"

"Let her be," says Mister Beale, rescuing me. "She's promised not to go too far. Let her be."

"She's motherless. My duty to see her right." Missus Beale, lips pressed thin, isn't happy about her "duty." I wish she'd quit.

"Tomorrow, Sugar," she says sternly. "Tomorrow, we've got to get on with your chores."

Behind my back, I cross my fingers. "Tomorrow."

I'm not promising. Just repeating.

The Beales are snoring, deep and quivering. I hear it through the wall.

Not quite dawn, I wipe sleep from my eyes, then stand, grab my shawl, shoes, and tiptoe toward my door. I push gently. The hinge squeaks, and cold creeps across my face.

Toe, heel, toe, heel, I reach the bottom porch step.

"Sugar!" Missus Beale is fuming, her face red. Her eyes are sharp, black like a beetle's. "There's work to do."

I tremble. My feet won't move as Missus Beale starts down the steps to snatch me.

"Eugenie," pleads Mister Beale from the door. "Let her go, Eugenie." His voice sounds so forlorn. "Let her be a child. You wanted the same for our children."

Missus Beale's eyes water. I'm not sure why. Turning, she reaches for Mister Beale's hand.

I take off running. I know Missus Beale loves Mister Beale. She just doesn't love me.

"Sugar! You come back here," shouts Missus Beale.

I keep running.

I run to the riverbank. The ground is grassy, squishy. "Billy. Billy!" His yellow curly head pops up. He'd been lying so still, I couldn't see him. "You made it!"

"'Course I did," he answers. "I tied my tutor's foot to the bed. When he wakes, he's going to holler something mad."

"Your folks, too?"

"Yep. Ma's fuming. Says I'll never be a gentleman. Pa says he's gonna whip me if I miss another lesson. But he won't."

"Why?"

"Says 'moderation.'"

"What's that mean?"

"I don't know. I only know he thinks I shouldn't study all the time."

"Moderation," I say gaily. "Like Mister Beale thinks I shouldn't work all the time."

Billy looks at me funny, his eyes squinting, his skinny arms hanging loose.

"Missus Beale is like your ma. 'Work, work, work.' No time for fun."

Billy squints, like he's trying to see me better. Maybe he thinks I have freckles, too?

"Pirates," he exclaims. "Let's be pirates. Pirates make their own rules." He leaps, dashes off. "Come on, Sugar. Come on!"

I run after him, feeling Ma running beside me. Feeling free.

"Look," says Billy, though I'm not sure at what. There's a bend in the river. Rough and quick, he pulls back bushes, branches. "Our raft. Me and Anthony built it."

The raft is the sorriest thing I ever saw. Mismatched pieces of gray crackling logs strapped with moldy rope. Two people could barely fit.

"I'm not getting on that."

"You have to, if you're going to play pirates."

I stare at the raft. Brown river water laps all over it. "It won't float."

"Will, too. It's floating now. All I got to do is untie the rope. And we're off. Hunting treasure."

"I don't know," I say, low. I don't tell Billy I can't swim. Splashing close to shore in shallow water is all I know.

"Scared?"

"No." But I am. "I'm captain."

"Girls aren't captains."

"Then I won't go."

"I never get to be captain," squeals Billy. "Anthony's always captain."

"No turns?"

"No," says Billy, shaking his head. "I'm always crew."

I should be nice and polite, say, "Billy, let's take turns." But if I'm going to risk my life, I want to drown as captain.

"We'll both be captains."

"Ahoy," crows Billy.

"Ahoy," I holler, not knowing what *ahoy* means.

Floating feels finer than anything I ever imagined. I'm not tied to land, sugarcane. My heart beats fierce. Even though the raft keeps close to shore, I feel a fine tingling of fear.

Billy uses a long branch to keep mud, muck, and plants from dragging the raft down. The Mississippi just pulls us along. The river's nice, lapping at the wood, gentle-soft.

On the water, I feel how big the river is! Wide, long, and deep. I can't see bottom. That scares me. But I see fish I've never seen up close and alive. I see a silvery bass, a carp, even a fat catfish, before it dives and disappears. Mister Beale's fish are always gutted dead.

Over his shoulder, Billy looks at me. "Isn't it fine, Sugar?"

"It's fine, Billy Wills." No grown-ups yelling, just me and Billy, floating. Smelling river air, balancing, as the raft bobs. I think this must be what freedom is. On the river, hearing water while a soft wind strokes your cheek. Seeing blue sky, bright sun, and a horizon that never ends.

Wordless, Billy points. A white egret soars. Billy jabs at muck and grass. He's not as strong as me, but he steers fine. I relax, feeling the best I've felt since Ma died.

Billy grins, shouts, "Want a turn?"

The branch is twirling, swirling in the deep, dark water. "You're doing fine. You be captain," I say.

I don't say, *I like being scared. But not too scared.*

In the river's middle, I see white-crested waves and ripples; beneath, I think, are wild and invisible currents. There the river runs faster. There I know our raft would bob, flip, and drown. I bite my lip.

Still, body swaying, hearing the *whoosh-whoosh* waves, seeing land pass by, the empty cane fields, I feel happy, free. Then I remember Billy's secret about Chinamen crossing the sea.

As if he knew what I was thinking, Billy murmurs, "Won't be long, Sugar. The Chinamen are coming."

The sun hides behind clouds. I can't help it. I shiver.

꒰ꔫ꒱

Lizzie's watching us from shore, her face and fists tight.

"You're going to be in so much trouble!" She's not

looking at me; she's looking at Billy. But she's talking to me. A jump rope dangles from her hand.

"Hey, Lizzie. Come help." She runs forward and helps us drag the raft into the cove. Mud sucks at the wood; water slaps it.

"We've got to hide it," says Billy, tossing branches and bush leaves on the raft.

And like she did it every day, Lizzie helps. We wedge the raft into river grass and dirt. Finished, all three of us smile.

"Lizzie, want to play?"

"Not with him," she says.

"I don't want to play with you, either," says Billy. "Pa says blacks are less than nothing."

I crinkle my brows. Billy doesn't believe what his pa says, does he?

"If you weren't Mister Wills's son, I'd kick you."

"Pa would have you whipped."

I think Lizzie's really going to do it—kick Billy.

Usually, Billy's nice. Lizzie, too. But Lizzie's trying to protect me and Billy's not used to back talk. Both look like skunks ready to fight.

37

I step between them. "Stop. We'll all get in trouble. Pretend nothing happened."

Billy scowls; he looks as mean as his pa.

"Billy, please. For me."

Billy glares. He blinks, uncurls his fists, and stomps off.

I turn to Lizzie. I want to hug her—my brave, best friend. Instead, I say, "Don't tell, Lizzie."

"He can't be your friend. White folks are different. They have their place. We have ours."

I follow Lizzie back to our shacks. Dirt doesn't swirl or make sounds like water. Sailing down the river, me and Billy were both pirates.

The same.

A Story for Ma

New Year's Day, I hide beneath an evergreen. Boughs hang down like curtains. Lying on my elbows and belly, I feel safe and warm, smell crisp and clean. Dry and fresh needles scratch my legs and arms. It's quiet. Cozy dark.

A perfect place to remember Ma.

"Being comfortable isn't everything," Ma would say. "Life's hard. But still you've got to find joy where you can."

Two years ago today, Ma died.

*   *   *

Last days before she died, Ma fretted, "I'll be getting up soon. Just need rest, Sugar. A little rest."

"I love you, Ma."

"Your pa will come back. I just know it. No matter what—you stay put."

I did stay put. I kept my promise. But I've been waiting and waiting, and Pa still hasn't come. I don't know what to do.

Nights, fever burned in Ma. Sometimes she didn't make sense. Sometimes she talked "sorry" talk. Sorry for staying at River Road, for Pa being sold. Sorry for me working cane. "Sorry I got sick," she whispered, hoarse. "But we fooled Mister Wills. We kept the secret. Didn't we, Sugar?"

My first big secret.

I sit up, feeling my chest tightening. Tree bark scratches me. Pine needles cling to my hair.

I hated our secret. Knowing each time Ma swung her machete, she gritted her jaw in pain. Inside her, something was wrong. We didn't tell anybody. But I think Missus Beale guessed. Ma didn't tell anyone in case Mister Wills found out.

"I don't pay for sick folks to cheat me of honest labor," Mister Wills says. Except he is the one who cheats, steals. One sick day and he withholds the whole season's pay.

After collecting last year's dollars, Ma lay down and didn't get up again. To comfort her, I told stories. Rubbed her feet. Placed cool rags on her brow. She'd repeat, "We kept our secret, didn't we?" I'd answer, "Yes, Ma. We kept our secret."

Two days before Ma died, her mind was calm. She spoke, clear. "Do. See. Feel." Then she closed her eyes. She died without ever seeing me again.

Exhaling, I wipe my eyes.

Hugging my knees to my chest, I whisper, "Ma. Do you still like stories?"

The branches shudder. Morning dew shimmers, and a worm inches over pine.

I think about Mister Beale's special stories. "Ma? Br'er Rabbit is the best trickster. He makes me laugh."

I hold my breath. I hear bells. Not the harsh

clang of the cowbell on the plantation, but something more delicate, tinkling. Maybe it's Ma, answering me?

I tell her a story. Tell her how Br'er Rabbit isn't really lazy. He just doesn't like being told what to do. Doesn't like masters, or orders. Being smart and tricky makes him happy. Br'er Rabbit's free.

Evening, I find a plate of black-eyed peas and collards at my door. Collards are supposed to bring good-luck dollars in the new year. The peas bring coins. As far as I know, it doesn't work. Still, each year, everybody eats them.

My stomach growls. I lift the plate. The Beales' door opens slightly.

"Thank you, Missus Beale."

Missus Beale doesn't answer. She softly shuts the door.

I add kindling to the log in the fireplace and strike flint to make a spark.

I scrape collards and peas into a pot and hang it on the fire hook.

Manon and Annie only cook for cane workers during harvest.

"Cooks work hard. But cooking doesn't wear the body down," Ma would say. "Not like sugar."

Cooks never stink of dirt. Manon and Annie have a shack near the big house. They live better than us in the old slave yard. Quieter. Cleaner. They were given to Missus Wills when they were little girls. I hear they don't have dirt floors but wooden planks. They even have a window.

My shack is windowless. The space is ten steps forward, back, and sideways. Very small.

I eat my peas, chewing them to mash before swallowing.

I wish Ma could've been a cook. Maybe she wouldn't have died. Collards slide down my throat. Only juice is left on the plate.

I feel better. Full.

"Thank you, Missus Beale," I whisper into the air.

Maybe she didn't answer because she didn't know what to say.

I know what to say.

I feel like a skunk in a trap.

How come I'm not really free?

Left Behind

It's morning and the sun looks like a wobbly egg yolk in the sky. The air is flinty green. Gray clouds are disappearing.

Me and Mister Beale are sitting on the porch steps.

The Beales were a wall away when I was born.

"You were fussy even then. Screamed all day, all night," Mister Beale tells me. He's smiling. I wrap my hand around his tough leather hands. I love to hear about when I was born.

"You had spunk."

"Still do," I say.

He gently taps my nose. "Tell me what trouble you've been into."

"Really?" Mister Beale is the only one who likes to hear my tales. I wish I could tell him about Billy.

Mister Beale blinks. He's waiting, hoping I'll make him laugh, erase the tiredness and sadness from his face.

I say, my voice low, "I pulled a tail feather from Rooster Ugly."

"No!"

"Yes," I say, poking out my chest. Rooster Ugly, scrawny, with red eyes, is as mean as they come. "Ugly pecked at the littlest hen."

"The one you call Peanut?"

"Yes. Peanut wasn't doing nothin'. Just eating grain. Ugly pecked her. So I pecked Ugly. Plucked his feather!"

"Did he chase you?"

"Yes. But I ran faster. Climbed a tree."

"Can't have Rooster Ugly pecking at Peanut." He shakes his gray head. "Not right."

"That's right."

"What else'd you do?"

Mister Beale's eyes have clouds inside them. He sees me, but not so well. One day he says I'll disappear; the clouds will make his eyes see nothing but white. He says when that happens, my tales will comfort him.

Missus Thornton walks by. She sniffs. Her hips boom back and forth like sticks beating on a drum. Mister Petey, who's almost as nice as Mister Beale, tips his hat. Missus Thornton still sniffs as if he's done wrong.

I scoot closer to Mister Beale. "I laid a cage for a skunk. I'm going to catch one!"

"What're you going to do with it?"

I mumble.

"What?"

I mumble louder. "Give it to Missus Thornton."

Mister Beale falls down laughing. "She'll be cleaning her house for a week." He sits up, wiping tears from his eyes. "You know you're not supposed to be playing pranks on grown folks."

"I know. I can't help myself. If Ma were still here, I'd be a worry to her."

"A fine worry," Mister Beale says. Then he looks far off, with his blurry, bleary eyes.

I know he's missing his children. Late at night, missing children is all Mister and Missus Beale talk about. They wonder what it's like up north. If their children are happy, earning money. If they made a mistake not traveling north.

I don't think they know I can hear. But the wall between us is thin, and, most nights, I stay awake for hours imagining me, Ma, and Pa together again.

Missus Beale always speaks the last words. "I wonder if our children have children."

I scoot closer to Mister Beale. "Were you spunky, too?" It's hard to imagine Mister Beale as a boy, as young as me.

"Snakes," Mister Beale says, nodding. He roars with laughter, and I see all his upper teeth. Some white, some yellow, some just gone. "I put snakes everywhere. Clothes. Baskets. Huts."

"In Africa?"

"Yes. Before I was captured." His hands grip his knees. "Slaves have no time for play." His eyes look sad again.

Wanting to distract him, I say, "Tell me a tale. About Hyena and Rabbit."

"I've told you a hundred times."

"All the more reason for you two to get to work." Missus Beale is standing in the doorway, an apron covering her skirt and tummy, and a drying cloth in her hands. "Sugar already has too many fancies in her head. It isn't natural."

Me and Mister Beale both sigh.

"I'd like to hear a story," says Lizzie.

"Where'd you come from?" I ask.

Lizzie is standing right before us, in her best shift, the one without any holes. She has a bundle in her arms. Something wrapped tightly in her shawl.

Mister and Missus Beale look funny at each other.

"What's going on?" I ask.

Mister Beale clears his throat and says, "Story time."

I clap. Lizzie sits beside me on the step. She holds

my hand. It feels good. Before her crush on Mo Johnson, we used to hold hands all the time. Play jump rope and tic-tac-toe.

"Br'er Rabbit was a trickster. Liked to think he could outwit anybody."

Like magic, folks start gathering. Everybody loves Mister Beale's stories.

"Now, you all know this here tale came from Africa," says Mister Beale. "In Africa, there're hyenas. Bigger than a fox, wilder than any rabid dog. My father told me this story. Now I'm telling you.

"Hyena and Rabbit were fighting, fussing brothers. Hyena even wanted to eat Rabbit. But Br'er Rabbit wasn't perfect. He thought he was the center of the world. Too, too proud."

"Like some folks I know," says Missus Thornton, staring straight at me.

"Hyena made a Tar Baby. A rag doll with big eyes. Curly hair. And floppy ears like Rabbit. He painted it with sticky tar and turpentine."

"He set a trap," shouts Lizzie.

"That's right. A trap for proud Rabbit!"

"Rabbit walked by Tar Baby," says Missus Thornton.

"And said 'hello,'" calls Reverend.

"But Tar Baby didn't answer back," I shout.

"No, sirree," says Mister Beale. "Br'er Rabbit says to Tar Baby, 'Maybe you didn't hear me? I said, "Hello."'

"Tar Baby said nothing.

"'Maybe you're a stranger here? Maybe you don't know it's rude not to speak when spoken to? I've got good manners. You should, too!' Br'er Rabbit punched Tar Baby, right in the mouth. His hand stuck!

"'Let me go,' screamed Br'er Rabbit. Hyena was rolling on the ground with laughter.

"The harder Rabbit fought, the more he stuck to Tar Baby. They rolled and rolled in the dirt. 'Pity, pity poor me,' cried Rabbit.

"'Got you, got you at last,' crowed Hyena, jumping out from his hiding place. 'I'm going to eat you for supper.'"

"What Rabbit do?" shouts Lizzie.

"On his hind legs, Rabbit drew himself tall, his front paws clasped together. He would've looked dignified, if tar hadn't smudged his gray fur black, if Tar Baby wasn't wrapped around his body with a silly smile.

" 'You've won, Hyena. You've won. Cook me with carrots and onions in the pot. I'll go down easy. I promise not to upset your stomach.'

" 'That's mighty kind of you, Br'er Rabbit.'

" 'I know when I've been bested,' Rabbit sniffed. 'But whatever you do, please don't throw me in the briar patch.' "

"Can I tell this part? Please, Mister Beale?" I leap onto the top step. "The briar patch was Rabbit's home. Rabbit was used to all its thorns, its prickly plants. Prickly like sugarcane. 'Just have mercy,' he said." I clutch my hands in prayer, just like Br'er Rabbit clutched his paws, and with all the drama I could muster, yell, " 'Please, please, *pleassssse*, don't throw me in the briar patch.' "

Lizzie claps.

Mister Beale crows, "Hyena was *dee*-lighted! He'd finally caught Br'er Rabbit!

"'Br'er Rabbit, you've fooled, tormented me for years. Time for you to pay for all your tricks.' He gripped Rabbit by the neck and tossed him in the briar patch.

"The briar patch was just what Rabbit wanted. Soon as Br'er Rabbit landed in the prickly patch, he twisted and twisted until the prickles stuck hold of Tar Baby's head, arms, body, and legs. Then Rabbit pulled himself free. 'Unstuck,' he chortled to Hyena. 'You silly fool. Can't catch me. I'm free!'

"Hyena stomped and stormed, howled and growled. For, once again..." Mister Beale pauses.

Everybody chants, "Trickster Rabbit outsmarted the powerful but dumb Hyena!"

We all laugh, some holding stomachs, some slapping thighs, me giggling, and Lizzie using her hands to cover her smile.

"That was fine, Mister Beale," I say. "Real fine. Tell another. Please. Please. *Pleassssse*."

"Time to go," shouts a voice, sounding from far,

far off. I turn my head, trying to figure out where the voice is coming from. Lizzie's not smiling. Mister Beale hangs his head. It's like all the joy got sucked right out of the yard.

"Time to go." It's Lizzie's pa. He's stout with bow-legs, and he's walking toward us. The crowd in front of the porch parts. I can see Lizzie's ma on the wagon perch. Her brothers are in the back, leaning against mattresses, a wooden chest, empty kerosene lamps, and stacks of quilts and linens.

Mister Wright extends his hand.

Lizzie stands, clutching her shawl against her chest.

"What's in there?" I point.

"My things. Clothes. Hair ribbons."

"Come on," says Mister Wright.

My eyes widen. "You're leaving?"

"Going north." Lizzie's face is calm—so calm I can't let myself cry.

"We're going to St. Louis."

"Where the Johnsons went?"

"Lizzie!"

She clutches her pa's hand. "Got to go," she says.

Then she breaks from her pa's clasp, dashes up the steps, and hugs me tight.

I hold on to her. Tight, tighter. I feel her body trying to move away, and I can't let go. "What will I do without you?" I whisper.

Missus Beale grabs my shoulders and gently pulls me from Lizzie.

"Be happy for me," says Lizzie.

There's a big rock in my throat.

Lizzie scampers onto the wagon. Filled with straw baskets of food. River Road folks always give what they can—preserves, biscuits, dried beans—to folks going north.

How'd I miss it? The loading of the wagon? They must've been doing it all last night and this morning.

How did I not know what everybody else knew? Lizzie, her ma and pa were leaving. Going north.

I holler, "Mister and Missus Wright! Please take me. Please. I'll be good." Mister Beale is holding me back. "Better than good. Please."

Lizzie's ma looks straight ahead.

"Hey ya," says Lizzie's pa. The mangy horse jerks,

the wagon wheels roll. Lizzie's body rocks forward and back. She is holding on to her shawl. There's a ribbon in her hair. I didn't notice that, either.

I twist from Mister Beale's grasp, leap off the steps, and start running. "I'm happy for you, Lizzie. I'm happy." As fast as I run, that old horse runs faster. Just keeps going while I lose all my breath.

"I'm happy," I shout. But I'm crying, too.

Lizzie waves and waves. I stop running. She keeps waving, her body rocking with the wagon. I watch until I can't see her no more.

Lizzie is gone forever and ever.

Like everybody else who went north. Like everybody else who left me behind.

Okra for the Chinamen

I miss Lizzie. I haven't seen Billy all week. Maybe Mister Wills found out we played? Maybe Billy no longer likes me?

Missus Beale comes onto the porch, flapping her dishrag at me. "Get busy, Sugar. Tend the garden."

"I hate it here."

"Hush, Sugar."

"Why didn't you go north?"

"Don't question me. You're a child. Do as you're told. Be hush. Work."

"I can't," I insist, my heart racing.

Missus Beale glares sternly and crosses her arms. *How come grown folks always win?*

I feel an imp overtaking me. I jump, stomp. "Nobody asked me if I wanted to be here."

Missus Beale looks at me like I've lost my mind, like I'm a chicken running around the yard with its head cut off.

"Mister Beale," she hollers. "Come tame this child."

Arms flailing, I kick up dirt, making dust. I know I'm behaving badly, but I can't help myself. Unhappiness, like a wildfire, is burning inside me.

Even Mister Beale has a "pity-pity" look on his face. His look scares me.

*How come*s start spilling out of me: "How come no one tells me nothin'? How come Lizzie's got to go? How come north is far? How come it can't be close? What's so good about the North, anyway?"

"You're not making any sense," says Missus Beale. "North is what it is."

I scrunch my lips. What I really want to say is *I'm tired of staying at River Road. How come I can't fly away? Cruise the river on a steamship?*

Instead, I fuss. "How come Mister Wills pays *after* harvest? How come I make less?"

"'Cause you're a child," Missus Beale says flatly.

"How come I've got to pay rent? I hate this old shack." I toss dirt at the steps.

"That's what freedom is," says Mister Beale.

My eyes fill with tears. Everything's a blur. I can't see. "Nobody asked me if I wanted this kind of free."

"Time to garden," grunts Missus Beale. "Folks got to live. Shelter, food, that's more than some got."

Mister Beale, on his beanpole legs, walks down the steps and holds me. I wiggle, squirm. But he keeps holding me.

"Sugar, Sugar, Sugar."

I can't move. Can't twist away. His arms remind me of Ma's arms, strong, tighter than a braid.

"I'm fine," I say.

His arms release me.

I wipe my eyes and nose. Mister Beale looks worried. Like it's his fault that I'm so sad.

I swallow. Mister Beale is the nicest person I know.

Seeing myself in his cloudy eyes, I think I'm a too, too sad picture.

Missus Beale is frowning, flapping her apron like a flag. I know she's worried about me, too.

I breathe deep. Mister and Missus Beale have enough sorrow.

"I'm going to go bald," I say.

"What?" squeaks Missus Beale.

"My hair is going to fall right out! That's what Ma used to say. That's what comes from complaining. 'Your hair falls right out.'" I scratch my head. "Any day now, I suspect I'll wake up bald."

Mister Beale laughs.

Missus Beale says, "Fancies. My word. Your head is full of fancies." She wraps her arms around me and nearly smothers me.

She holds me at arm's length. "Your ma was a fine woman, and she loved you."

I blink, about to cry again. I fling myself into Missus Beale. I cling to her waist, pressing my face against her, all soft and warm.

"Now, now," says Missus Beale, pulling away. "Time

for work. No more foolishness. Got to get our spring garden in. *Humph.*"

Her face is all frumpy-grumpy again. I don't feel bad. Missus Beale hugged me. She never hugged me before.

"Gardening isn't hard," I say. "It's easy compared to cane. I'm not going to complain no more."

"That's my Sugar. My sugar girl," says Mister Beale.

"Look at me, Missus Beale." I try to spin my legs high in the air like Billy did. My knees bend like a bug's.

Missus Beale claps. Then, ever practical, she grunts, "Get to work."

"I'll tell you a story later," says Mister Beale, picking up his cloth bag filled with seeds.

"About Chinamen?" I blurt.

He spins, looks at me fierce. I clap hands over my mouth. I've never seen Mister Beale so angry. Missus Beale's lips press thin, tight.

"Where'd you hear about Chinamen?"

"Don't be mad at me. Please."

A look passes between Mister and Missus Beale. I

61

don't understand it. But Missus Beale's shoulders slump, and she looks older than the old she is.

"I'm not mad at you, Sugar," Mister Beale says softly.

"Get the garden in," says Missus Beale, her voice like a stone.

Mister Beale nods at Missus Beale. He extends his hand. I take it. We walk toward our garden. I'm itching with disgust. I'm no good. I didn't keep Billy's secret. More awful, I made Mister Beale angry. I worried the Beales.

"Sugar, let's make a fine garden. What vegetable do you want most?"

"Extra peas, please." But I don't really care. I know Mister Beale is just talking to talk. Grown folks do that—talk when they're upset. Or else don't talk at all, if they're worse than upset.

I guess this is good. Mister Beale is talking.

But underneath his chatter about peas, beans, corn, I hear, even though he doesn't say it, *Chinamen are not a good thing.*

But are they bad?

I wonder if Chinamen are anything like Africans. I wonder if they'll look like Mister Beale. Or me? Does China have hyenas? Rabbits and lions?

To Mister Wills, Chinamen are important—more than "less-than-nothing" folks. Better than me?

We walk closer and closer to the garden dirt. I can see the cane fields, dirt that will grow green shoots, cane stalks waving in the breeze.

Awful, awful days of work to come!

I squeeze Mister Beale's hand. He squeezes back.

I wonder if Billy will ever play with me again.

"Let's get to work." Mister Beale hands me seeds. "No garden, and we won't have enough to eat."

I look at all the patches. Everyone has one. A tiny share of dirt to grow food. It isn't fair.

Mister Beale squats, planting peas. The Beales share their garden with me in exchange for work. When Ma died, Reverend and Missus Thornton took my garden. She said, "A child doesn't need so much! We'll share with those in need."

Reverend believes in sharing, but Missus Thornton, I think, eats too much. Her hips are wider than a gator.

I collapse onto my knees. Scrape away dirt, poke my finger down, and plant a seed.

When the Chinamen come, I'm going to give them nasty okra.

In the Briar Patch

I can't escape. Missus Beale watches me close, makes sure I do my chores. Every step I take, she's beside me. Every day, she's got new chores. Every day, she asks, "How'd you hear about Chinamen?"

I squirm, hem and haw, but I don't tell. Unsmiling, Missus Beale peers at me like she can see straight into my heart.

Three mornings in a row, she's met me on the porch steps before I can run off. Maybe Lizzie told her about me and Billy? Maybe she thinks I'll repent and tell her who told me about Chinamen?

"Soap today."

I hate making soap.

"Get the tallow pail," says Missus Beale, tying her blue apron.

Nasty! The tallow pail is filled with grease and pork fat. It's thick, grayish white.

A pot hangs over the yard fire. I hand Missus Beale the tallow. She pours the sluggish gopply-goop into the pot. It smells rancid, even worse than sugar.

"I hear Mister Beale calling," I say.

"No one's calling. Stir, Sugar."

I lift the rod and stir.

"Afterward, we're going to sew you a new shift."

"I really think Mister Beale's calling me. There. Can't you hear?"

"Sugar, stir!" Missus Beale pours in lye. Lye burns; my eyes water, my nose runs. If it gets on me, I'll scar.

I stir carefully. It'll take hours for the fat and lye to melt and mix. In my mind, I can see Billy climbing trees, see him floating on the raft. See him catching bugs. Even if he's studying, I still think Billy is having more fun than me.

I sniff. "Billy doesn't make his own clothes."

"No. The housemaid does."

"It isn't fair."

"Be happy you're free. They can't sell us anymore. At least you've got a cotton shift, not burlap."

I stop stirring. Plain misery. I might as well jump in the pot if I can't have adventures.

"Sugar." Missus Beale clutches my free hand. Both our hands are rough; hers are blotchy and wrinkled. "You got to learn to do for yourself."

"I know. 'Cause Ma's gone. And you're so old."

"I'm not going to die just yet," Missus Beale humphs.

Mournful, I shake my head side to side. "Missus Beale, you might die soon. You're already losing your hearing."

"What?!" Missus Beale shrieks.

"Mister Beale's in the garden, hollering for me. He really is. I'm so sorry. Real sorry, you can't hear."

I peek up. Frowning, Missus Beale is touching her ears.

"He's been yelling, 'Moderation. Moderation.'"

"Moderation? What's that mean?"

"Less chores!"

I start running.

Smack. I run into Missus Thornton! Hands on her hips, she blocks my way. "Apologize to Missus Beale."

I sigh. Turn. "I'm sorry, Missus Beale."

Missus Beale is very unhappy. I rock back on my heels, bow my head. "I'm mistaken, Missus Beale. Nobody's calling me."

I pick up the dropped rod.

Soap—who needs it? Sugar smells don't fade. Dirt never goes away.

Missus Beale makes me sit on the porch steps. I'm not allowed to do anything. Not even chores.

I count cracks in the wood. Search for spiders and ants in the dirt. Scratch the scabs on my knees. Untie and tie my pigtails. Try to guess how many clouds there are in the sky. Try to remember Ma loved me. Try to forget Lizzie. (She probably has a dozen new friends.) Try to forget Billy has a better life than me.

Worse, sitting on the steps, I see how slow the old folks shuffle. See their sad and worried faces. Hear their whispering. It's like our yard is filled with drowsy, fretting moths. Mister Petey is talking low with Mister Bailey. Reverend is whispering to Missus Ellie. Mister and Missus Beale grumble, scattering chicken feed. Even Missus Thornton is sewing on her porch, mumbling to herself.

I listen hard. "Chinamen." *Whisper-whisper-whisper.* "Chinamen."

It sounds like a storm rolling in from the horizon. *Mumble—whisper—rumble.* "Chinamen." Like gray, black clouds are sweeping in, making River Road folks uneasy.

"We're going to lose our jobs," they say. "Lose our homes." "Have to leave River Road."

Even though the day is bright, worry and fear are striking like invisible lightning and silent thunderbolts.

*　　*　　*

"Are you ready to work now?" Missus Beale asks. Her face is a map of wrinkles.

"Yes, ma'am."

"You've got to be practical, Sugar. Stop filling your head with stories. Use some sense."

"Yes, ma'am."

"Don't be thinking I wouldn't treat my daughter just the same."

"No, ma'am."

"Let's get to work."

I help Missus Beale pour the squishy, harsh soap into pans. When it cools, it'll harden, and we'll cut it into bars.

I shouldn't have tried to trick Missus Beale. It's just more fun acting like Br'er Rabbit.

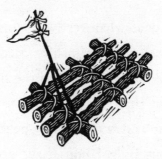

Pebbles

Since dawn, I've been standing outside the big house. I've gathered a handful of pebbles.

"Keep to your own." Nobody asked me what I thought. Or Billy. Why can't we decide for ourselves?

Still, doing something is better than doing nothing. Even though it's scary. But I can't let Missus Beale keep me close. I dreamed of me and Billy rafting.

I have to know: Does he still want to be friends?

No Name cat watches me. He's black with a white belly. Six toes on his paws. His eyes are curious, almost entirely black.

No Name does whatever No Name wants to do. He licks himself in the sunshine, sleeps as much as he wants, and hunts for mice in the sugar mill. He's got a better life than me.

I'm going to throw and throw pebbles until folks realize without Billy I don't have any adventures, any fun.

Missus Beale's going to be mad when she realizes I didn't sleep, that I slipped out in the dead of night to escape chores, to escape her.

Days were better when I had Ma. Working, doing chores, we'd smile. Laugh. Talk. Dream of better days. Without Ma, shouldn't I be trying to make days better?

If Ma were alive, I think she'd like Billy. She wouldn't mind me breaking rules. She'd understand me and Billy mix together, just fine.

I think, *Billy's following the rules.* He's not used to being in as much trouble as me.

I think, *He's forgotten we're pirates.* "Pirates don't follow rules."

*   *   *

Billy's room is on the second floor, on the far right corner. I've never been inside, but I've seen him poking his head out the window.

I pick up a pebble and throw. It doesn't even hit the house.

I throw another pebble. It hits closer to Billy's window.

No Name meows.

I throw again. The pebble hits the window frame. I hold my breath. Nothin'! Billy doesn't wake up.

I throw, another and another.

Clawing, No Name rolls my pebbles.

"Scat," I say. Then, picking up a handful of pebbles, I throw. *Crack. Crack. Crack.* Pebbles bounce off the house and window. Still Billy doesn't wake up.

I grab a rock and throw. The window breaks. I hear shouts, screams from Mister and Missus Wills.

Through the broken glass, Billy looks down. I wave.

"Sugar!" Mister Wills yells from a window on the left. "I'm going to tan your hide."

I take off running.

*   *   *

I run to the river, slip off my shoes, and start kicking up waves.

Behind me, I hear footsteps, grunts as Billy falls to the ground, kicking off shoes. He stands. Together we kick up waves.

I bend, scoop up muddy water, and toss it at Billy.

Billy shakes his head, sending water and mud flying.

I hold my breath. *Will he be angry?*

Billy hoots, smiling, like a burst of light, "Come on, let's fight."

Gleeful, I don't duck when Billy splashes me. Water and river mud drip down my face and shift.

We splash and splash like we're trying to empty the river. Billy rushes close. Stooping, he scoops up a mountain of water. I can't see! The Mississippi is filling my eyes, soaking my hair.

"Oh," I explode. I chase Billy down the shoreline. He zigs, zags; so do I. Mud sucks at our feet, making smacking sounds. Billy turns, runs onto shore. Chest heaving, he collapses, saying, "You . . . win."

Billy is covered with mud. Breathing, but not as hard as he is, I fold my legs beneath me. "You're a mess."

He answers, "You should talk."

We giggle.

"I've been meaning to tell you. A hyena is like a big, dumb fox. It lives in Africa."

Billy sits up, his eyes bright. "'Rabbits are smart. Hyenas are dumb,' you said." He wrinkles his nose. "Are you saying I'm dumb?"

"I thought you were. But now I think you're smart, a rabbit like me."

The sky is clearest blue, except for a streak, a white ribbon cloud. I wish I could sail on it. Just float away. I'd find another cloud for Billy.

Still, I'm uneasy. Waking Billy is the worst thing I've ever done. I bite my lip.

I ask what I've always wanted to ask. "Billy, what's beyond River Road?"

"Malveaux Plantation is far north. South is the DeLaviers Plantation. They plant flowers, too. At least a quarter acre. Pa says it's a waste of good cane land."

"Will you take me? To the DeLaviers'?" I want to see flowers, growing, on purpose.

"It'll take a while. Hours, rafting."

"An adventure. You be captain."

"Ahoy," crows Billy.

Rafting is better than I remember. Waves and currents lull, making me think of Ma. How holding each other, we danced and swayed.

Water rushes over wood, tickling me and Billy's legs and feet. There's a whole water world beneath us. Catfish, turtles, bluegills, and all kinds of small and large creatures I can't see.

On water, seeing algae clinging to our raft, I feel special. A bug-eyed fish blinks. My heart beats in time with the lapping waves. A flock of blackbirds shoot like arrows across the blue, white-speckled sky.

I can't live in water. I can't live in the sky. But thanks to Billy, I'm living *on* water.

As if I called his name, Billy turns his head and smiles. I think, *If he's really my friend, he won't say a word*. He'll know that this moment—here, now, skimming across water—is perfect.

Billy's mouth opens. His teeth are even, white. Then he closes his lips, faces forward. I sigh, content.

Our raft curves with the river. "There," says Billy. A patch of green bushes, a few green shoots poke through dirt. "Nothing's flowering yet. Come summer, this will be filled with red, yellow, blue, and white flowers. You'd like it, Sugar."

Behind the garden, I see fallow fields waiting for cane.

"Get your pole."

I lift the pole and dig it in the muck. In unison, me and Billy pull and lift, pull and lift, maneuvering the raft to shore.

Billy leaps off the raft, extends his hand. "Come on, Sugar."

I step, for the first time, on dirt that's not River Road. I can't help it. I cry.

Billy pretends not to see.

"Tomorrow?" I ask. The sun is low, orange-red, making the clouds glow. We're back at River Road.

"It'll be harder to escape." Billy finger-combs his hair, dirtying it more. "We're in such trouble."

"Everyone's always mad at me." Instead of feeling carefree, I feel sad.

"Ma and Pa have strange notions. They'd rather I be lonely than play with you. If I like you, why can't I play with you?"

I don't answer.

"I'm going to tell the Beales," I say, determined. "Mister Beale will be disappointed. Missus Beale might punish me. Might make me get a switch." I shake myself. "No secrets no more, Billy. I'm tired of them. Secrets are too much like lies."

"Pa wanted to keep the Chinamen secret. I overheard him talking to Mister Tom. Saying Chinamen was going to solve his problems. Him and Mister Tom started arguing. 'Change,' Pa kept saying. 'It's here. Whether we like it or not.' Mister Tom cursed. Slammed the door."

"Why'd you tell me, Billy? About Chinamen?"

"Didn't seem right not to. 'Sides, I always wanted to play with you. And Lizzie, Mo, Ulysses. But 'specially you. Seemed you liked adventures.

"All I had was Anthony. Ma says Anthony's going to be a gentleman. He's not a gentleman with me. He's tough, mean. He never wanted a brother."

I feel sorry for Billy. Once, I had lots of friends. Then, I had only Lizzie. Billy had no one, except a brother who didn't like him.

"Billy, I don't think we're bad."

"Me, either."

Billy cocks his head. "I wish I'd known you sooner, Sugar."

"So do I." I quiver, hold my breath as Billy extends his hand.

Our hands wrap together like the colors on the finger trap. My hand is scratchy, tough; his hand, smooth, soft. Billy grimaces, like seeing a black and a white hand shaking isn't right. I'm not sure it is, either.

But we both hold on.

Billy looks at me, serious, his blue eyes piercing like sky through a storm. "Next time," he says, "let's do blood."

I swallow. "Yes."

Billy chortles, dashing off. "Pa's going to be mad. Ma, madder!" Saying it, Billy sounds happy.

I'm happy, too. I'm not alone. Two in trouble is better than one.

I holler, "Billy. Next time, don't sleep so heavy!"

Punishment

Oh, no. Mister Wills is on our porch! Right in the workers' quarters!

Everybody's outside—dinner, chores stopped—milling in the yard, like bees to honey, watching Mister Wills meet with Mister Beale.

Faces are grim. Missus Beale digs her nails into her palms.

"Can't have it, Jem. Keep her"—Mister Wills points at me—"away. Keep her with her own kind."

"Yes, sir."

I blurt, "I like Billy. We just want to be friends."

Missus Beale pinches my arm.

"If you were still a slave, I'd have you whipped," says Mister Wills. "I still might have you whipped." He has Billy's bright blue eyes, but his face is snarling. His skin is creased, rough.

"You're on this property because I allow you to be. All of you," he says, turning, his hands flailing. "Any time, I can order you off my land.

"Tell me why I should shelter Sugar? She's a menace."

"It's hard without Sugar's ma," says Mister Beale. "I promise, we'll keep a closer eye."

"You do that. That's what we agreed, Jem. Otherwise, I'll run her off. You, too, if I must."

I'm shivering, frightened, furious at the same time.

Mister Wills and Mister Beale glare. Even though Mister Beale is old, he looks tough. Like he won't back down. He's skinny, tall; Mister Wills is short and round.

Mister Beale says, "I'll take care of Sugar."

Mister Wills thinks for a moment. "Someone has to pay for the window."

Mister Beale, angry, nods at Missus Beale. She goes inside the shack.

"How much?"

"A dollar."

"A dollar?" I gawk.

"Hush, Sugar," says Mister Beale. Missus Beale hands him a mostly empty jar. He fishes for a dollar.

"I'm sorry," I say. "I'm sorry, Mister Wills. I've got dollars. Mine and Ma's. Let me pay."

Missus Beale grips my shoulder, stops me from getting my money jar. "This is between the men, Sugar. Your money's your future."

Sorrier than I've ever been, I hang my head. I didn't mean to hurt Mister and Missus Beale.

"Just 'cause slavery's ended doesn't mean blacks, whites are equal," says Mister Wills.

"And Chinamen?" asks Mister Beale. "They equal?"

Mister Wills is surprised, caught off guard. Scowling, River Road folks grumble.

"No disrespect. Will Chinamen help your profit?"

"Yes, Chinamen," booms Mister Wills. "I need workers. Need to expand my crop. Times are hard.

During the war, Union soldiers burnt crops. The stable and the mill."

"We gonna lose our jobs?" asks Mister Waters.

"Cane work is all I know," shouts Missus Celeste. "River Road is all I know."

Missus Ellie weeps, "Don't got nobody. Nothing." Reverend comforts her.

"Jem," says Mister Wills, turning to Mister Beale. "We've known each other for a long time. You saw me grow up. Gave me my first taste of cane. But I'll run you and everyone else off if you question my judgment. Do your work—that's all I care about. I expect you and the Chinamen to work hard. I've always been a fair man."

I think, *Not true.* Else Ma might still be alive. When we were slaves, Mister Wills never stopped Mister Tom from lashing, yelling when folks' legs buckled or they fainted from heatstroke.

Now my heart's pounding. I'm ready to explode, thinking how unfair Mister Wills's been.

Mister Wills sold my pa.

"Jem, you keep your people in line. Else all of you can go. Leave River Road."

Our yard is crackling loud. Everybody's upset. But the porch is quiet, tense. Tight veins pop up on Mister Beale's neck. He and Mister Wills stare like no one else exists.

"We still work for you," says Mister Beale, his voice even. "You set the wages. Your right, but it's our right to worry about the future." Mister Beale pretends he's tipping a hat. "Good evening, Mister Wills."

"Good night, Jem."

I step forward. "'Night, Mister Wills." I want Mister Wills to see me. But even though his eyes are bulging wide, he doesn't. I want to tell him that I like Billy better than I like him. Instead, I curtsy. "I won't break windows no more."

Mister Wills thumps down the steps.

"When? When are they coming?" Mister Petey calls. River Road folks are circling, swarming about Mister Wills. "Chinamen. When they coming?" "When?"

Mister Wills doesn't look back, just shouts, ferocious, "Day after tomorrow."

Everyone, even Missus Beale, heads back to their shacks.

Mister Beale hasn't moved; he stands, straight back, looking out over the empty yard. Like the patch of dirt is his world, his home, his land. Like he's an African king.

The community fire is out. The yard, empty. I hear mice rustling, an owl hooting. I stare across the fields, flat, not furrowed. Fallow.

"I'm sorry, Mister Beale. I didn't mean to get you in trouble."

Mister Beale pats my head.

"I've got a dollar."

"You keep it, Sugar."

"You're always looking out for me."

"Everybody in River Road looks out for you."

I start unraveling my pigtail. "I know," I say, but I don't really. Folks always seem to wish I'd be quieter, obedient, uncomplaining.

"Ma said, 'Sugar's hard. Awful.'"

"That it is."

Then, bending on his knees, Mister Beale searches my face. "You're not talking about you, Sugar? Don't be thinking it. You're not awful. Your ma never meant that."

"I know." Though I still don't know why she named me Sugar. "When I was born, Ma said I smelled 'fresh.'"

"That's spunk, Sugar. It means you're you. You're bound to get in trouble."

"I don't mean to get in trouble. Don't mean to upset things. I just get restless."

"I lost spunk, Sugar," murmurs Mister Beale. "Lost it when they brought me here. To America. When I started working cane. Don't lose yours, Sugar. I don't think I could stand it. Can you try to get in a little less trouble?"

"I'll try. Sometimes, I just got to be spunky. I need to. Even when spunky is scary, like riding a raft—"

"When'd you do that?" Mister Beale asks sharply.

"Don't worry, Mister Beale, I didn't drown. Me and Billy had fun. Like Br'er Rabbit."

"Stay out of the river. Rafting's dangerous."

"I liked it."

"Sugar, do as I say," shouts Mister Beale, "or I'll tan your hide myself."

"Don't be angry, Mister Beale. Please." Tears are choking my voice.

Mister Beale stands. "As long as you work for Mister Wills, Sugar, you'll do as he says. No rafting. No Billy."

I stare at our shadows, lying, side by side, on the porch wood. Big shadow, small. Mister Beale moves.

The door opens and closes.

Only one shadow left. Mine.

Eagle Bright

I hide in bed.

Tomorrow, the Chinamen come. Yesterday, I got in so much trouble. The day after tomorrow is Planting Day. Cane season. Chinamen. Can't do nothin' about either.

Do Chinamen have big ears like Mo Johnson? Or yellow hair like Billy? I don't think they're going to like me.

They must be so brave to travel so far. Chinamen must be giants.

I sniff beneath the sheet, wipe my eyes with my arm.

I want to forget yesterday. Forget Mister Beale being mad.

I'd see Billy every day, even if I got in trouble. But I can't bring trouble to the Beales. Ma wouldn't want me to hurt them.

"Ma," I whisper, wishing she could answer.

But I know what she'd say. "As long as you can, Sugar, get up. Every day. Do. See. Feel." Mom got up until she couldn't.

She wouldn't want me to hide in bed.

So I throw off my sheet. Grab my shawl and slip on my shoes. I run, jumping off the porch, my arms outstretched like wings, shouting, "It's Eagle Day."

"Lord, lord," says Mister René, his gooseneck shaking.

"You've lost your wits," says Missus Thornton.

Even Mister Beale, rocking on the porch, looks at me quizzically. Grown folks mutter, murmur, "Silly child"; "No sense whatsoever"; "Just foolishness. Plain foolishness."

It's noon. I can't believe I wasted the morning hiding.

Just like I can't believe folks wasted all morning, moaning, groaning, saying harsh words about everything. Chinamen. The Willses. The weather, sugar. Me. Louisiana. The whole wide world.

I know eagles nest and birth in winter. Winter's dying, almost over. That's how we know it's time to plant cane. Eagle eggs should all be burst open.

Still, I'm hoping for magic. A miracle.

Ma said, "Miracles happen." That's why she believed Pa would come back one day. "He loves us, Sugar."

"I'm going to find an eagle's nest," I holler, loud and clear. "With eggs in it!"

Missus Thornton screeches, "Somebody ought to do something with that child!" She makes sure everyone hears her. She's pointing her finger at me. Making a ruckus. "She's wild. Needs a good licking."

The Reverend nods.

If Missus Thornton is going to make a fuss, I'll make a bigger one!

I start flapping my arms like wings.

Missus Thornton squawks, "Wild. Witless. Needs a spanking."

Then I splash water from the trough onto the ground. I make mud and plaster some on my face. I run in circles.

Missus Thornton faints, but I think she's pretending. The Reverend bends over her; all the busy-bee neighbors rush toward her and away from me.

On the porch, Missus Beale frowns. Mister Beale, his arms crossed, watches me.

"Bye, everyone! I'm off to hunt for eagles."

I race off.

I see steamboats churning water into foam.

I'm going to climb at least fifteen trees. One tree for each year I've been alive. Then five trees for the years I've been free.

Nothin'. Not a single bird. Just empty nests shaped with twigs. The nests are strong, heavy. Abandoned.

My legs and arms are scratched and tired. I'm angry I let the season pass without searching for an eagle.

Miracles don't happen. Pa didn't make it back after Mister Wills sold him. When slaves were freed, Ma kept saying for years, "Any day now, he'll be back."

But miracles don't happen. At least not to me.

I'm losing my spirit. Thirteen trees climbed, two more to go. I made a promise to myself: fifteen trees. So even though I don't want to, I do it! I dig my toes against bark, stretch my arm, and clutch a branch, then another and another. Dig toe, stretch arm. Bark tears at my shift. Ants scatter.

I feel the cypress breathing. It's an old tree, maybe older than River Road Plantation. Spanish moss hangs from its branches, all gray and swinging like clumps of rope. The leaves are shaped like feathers with tiny, spiked leaves.

I climb higher and higher. Higher than I've climbed before. There's a nest, its bottom tight with brown, gray twigs.

"Eggs, eggs," I whisper, hoping. "Waiting to be born."

But there aren't any eggs. The nest is empty.

*　　*　　*

I hear "*wee-aaaaaaaaa, wee-aaaaaaaaa.*" It's a bald eagle. Flying free.

Balancing in the tree's arms, I watch the bird circle, its brown wings wide, cutting through clouds and blue sky.

The bald eagle knows I'm watching it. Circling closer and closer to the cypress, its white head, tilting right, its beady, yellow eyes seeing me, I feel so very, very happy.

"*Wee-aaaaaaaaa.*" The eagle soars high, its wings and head sparkling. High, higher it flies until I have to close my eyes against the sun.

II

Planting

1871

Knee-How

T hey're here, they're here," Reverend Thornton shouts. Coming down the road, two
horses pull a wagon. I run fast to stand at
the front of the line.

All the River Road men line up, trying to look
fierce, strong. Like warriors. Except they're stick-
skinny in their baggy overalls.

Mister Wills is looking pleased with himself.

Overseer Tom just looks angry. He taps his whip
on his boot.

Anxious, I shuffle from foot to foot.

Mister Wills is pacing. Billy is on the big house porch. I wave. (I forgot I'm not supposed to know him.) He waves back. His ma, all bright and lacy, slaps his hand.

Horses *clop-clop*, then stop. The wagon has settled in the east side of the yard.

Mister Wills steps forward. "Welcome." His face beams.

"Get up," shouts the man next to the wagon's driver. He's lean, ugly. He jumps down from his seat, carrying a shotgun, and comes around, shouting at the two rows of men sitting on either side of the wagon. "Get up."

As one, the Chinamen stand.

They're short, with shiny black hair twisted in a braid down their backs. Their hair is longer than mine. They wear black caps. Their skin is warm, much lighter than mine, but sun-kissed in a nice way, not red and rough like Mister Wills's face. Their pants are billowy and loose. And even though it's so hot, they wear jackets that reach their knees and have sewn clasps on the front and a high-neck collar.

Billy's mouth is hanging open. Mine, too.

"Welcome," says Mister Wills.

The Chinamen move forward; there is a clanging, clinking sound. Mister Beale shouts, "What's this?"

Locks are closed around the Chinamen's ankles; chains link each man to the next. All the men— about a dozen—clamber down. The men try to right their balance, manage the distance the chains allow.

Mister Petey starts grumbling, "Not right. Not right at all."

Reverend Thornton says, "Lord a'mercy."

Mister Beale hollers, "No slaves no more. They shouldn't be chained. Nobody should be chained."

Mister Wills says nothing. His face looks puffy, red, like it's going to explode. The Overseer stretches his lips into an ugly smile.

"Had to chain them," says the wiry man, balancing his rifle. "Got to New Orleans and they wanted to change their minds. Imagine. Wanted to go back. To British Guiana. Like it was better than Louisiana. Said they didn't like the Americans they met on the ship. I called the law. Told them these yellow men were for Wills's plantation. They chained them nice. No one messes with Vincent Doucet. Felt good, felt like I was hauling slaves again." He juts out his hand. "Pay me now."

Mister Wills is furious. He reaches into his pocket and pulls out bills. I never saw so much!

The lean man counts the money.

"It's all there," says Mister Wills. "Unchain these men, Doucet. I want willing men. Willing workers."

"You didn't used to care about willing or unwilling," says Mister Tom.

"Slavery isn't returning, Tom. Like it or not, times are changing. Can't make a living without willing workers.

"Jem," Mister Wills shouts. "Lead these men to their shacks."

Mister Beale nods. "Yes, sir."

"My job's done," says Doucet. "I delivered your workers. Now I'm heading back to New Orleans."

"I'll not be hiring you again," says Mister Wills.

Mister Doucet snorts. "Going soft, Wills. Soon blacks and yellows will be running your plantation."

The Overseer, looking mean like a rattler, nods, agreeing.

"Dump their supplies in the yard," shouts Mister Wills to the wagon man. "Don't keep nothing that isn't yours."

Mister Beale unlocks the chained men.

I walk the length of the line. They're not big. But they look sad.

I remember Pa's chains, him being put on a wagon and carted off. Chains are awful. Like eagles with broken wings.

I come to the end of the line. None of the Chinamen looks at me. At least, I don't think so. Their heads are slightly bowed and their eyes seem to have curtains.

The last Chinaman has soft, black shoes. I stare at them. His shoes are better than mine.

"*Ni hao.*"

I look up.

"Knee-how." It's a whispery-soft, trilling sound.

The Chinaman's eyes are black, shaped like a leaf. "*Ni hao.*" He waves his hand, side to side.

"Knee-how," I say. We're saying hello.

The Chinaman winks.

"Come on," shouts Mister Beale. "Let's go."

"Cane time tomorrow," says Mister Wills with glee. "It's going to be a good harvest."

"Hard work," shouts the Overseer.

"Good riddance," says Doucet. "Chinamen, strange."

"Stubborn," says the driver, cracking the carriage whip. *Snap.* The horses jolt forward.

"I'll show you your quarters," says Mister Beale, waving his hands at the Chinamen. "Come."

The Chinamen follow. There are ten. Soft slippers moving, their pigtails swaying, they walk in a line like Mississippi ducks swimming after their mother or whooping cranes flying, following the lead crane over the marsh.

But the men aren't following Mister Beale, not really. They're following the sunburnt man beside him.

He's nodding at Mister Beale's words, his arms folded across his chest, his hands slipped inside his sleeves. I think he must be their leader. He's dignified, not as old as Mister Beale. The last man, the one who said "hello," is younger, maybe the youngest. But older than me and Billy. Watching him, the last in the line, I see him slip his fingers into a pocket and pull out something brown. He drops it.

No Name, who I thought was sleeping, pounces. He eats whatever it is and licks his paw.

Excited, Billy runs up beside me. "Isn't it amazing, Sugar?" Then he darts away before his pa can see him.

"Sure is," I say into the wind. I couldn't have imagined it. At River Road. New people called Chinamen.

Not black. Not white. A soft sun color in between.

❧

I splash water on my face, slip on my shoes, and step onto the porch. All the River Road folks are outside, frowning, standing on porches, in the yard, staring at our new neighbors.

Missus Beale cautions, "Be sensible, Sugar. Not too spirited."

"Why I never—"

Missus Beale peers, squints at me.

"Well, almost never." Then I gulp. "I won't."

Missus Beale doesn't understand me at all.

"I'm going to visit the Chinamen."

"No, Sugar," says Mister Beale. "We don't know what kind of people they are."

"That's what I want to find out," I call, leaping off the porch.

"Sugar, come here. Come back here." Mister Beale grabs my arm. "Get back to the porch right now."

"Why? I want to know about the Chinamen. Where they come from. How they live."

"Doesn't matter. If Mister Wills brought them, they don't mean us blacks any good."

"How do you know?"

Mister Beale glares. I can't stand the look on his face. Lowering my head, I wrap my arms about his waist. Mister Beale has been like a pa to me. But I don't think he's right. I used to think he was always right.

I can't be with Billy. Can't be with the Chinamen. "The middle of the yard," I plead. "Let me go there. Nothing can happen there. Please, Mister Beale."

"Not an inch closer."

* * *

I squat, halfway between our shacks and the China-men's shacks. I look at the dirt. Same dirt as yester-day. But now there's an invisible line. I feel chained, tied to a tether on a tree.

I look back. All the River Road folks look like ghosts. Pinched faces. Sour mouths. Clenching hands. They pretend to do work, eat, but really they're watching the Chinamen. And me.

Chinamen have smooth faces. They're unpacking bags, settling in. But they watch, too. One by one, sometimes two together, they straighten and stare over at us. They look strong. Not scary, not old. Just determined.

Nobody says anything. The sun dips lower in the sky.

I can't stand the strain, the scared and wary feel-ings in the air. I pop up, curtsy, and shout, "Knee-how."

In unison, Chinamen carol, "Ni hao. Ni hao." They bow, their chins touching their chests, folding like a tree bows in the wind.

I do it again. Curtsy. Shout. "Knee-how. Knee-how."

"*Ni hao. Ni hao.*"

I say "hello" five times. The Chinamen never ignore me. They stop washing clothes, digging a garden, or stirring greens in a pot. Even if they're sitting, resting on the porch, they stand and bow. "*Ni hao. Ni hao.*"

"Sugar," hollers Missus Beale. "Leave those men alone."

I roll my eyes.

Afternoon, the elder Chinaman puts a box on the porch. Men gather. *I want to see.* There's a pouch. Little round balls, like marbles—blue, white, and green—spill out.

I creep—toe, heel, toe, heel. Inch by inch, I cross the dirt, scooting closer to the Chinamen.

"Sugar!" Mister and Missus Beale shout.

Frustrated, I run back to the middle of the yard.

Sauntering past me, flicking his tail like he's better than me, No Name brushes against the youngest

Chinaman. He scoops him up. No Name goes limp, belly up. The Chinaman rubs his tummy.

He stares at me, dips his head toward No Name. He tickles him. No Name's head rolls back. *Funny cat.* I giggle. Without words, the Chinaman's talking to me. He squats, points to his pocket. He takes out something brown. Dried meat? He lifts his hand high; No Name leaps. I laugh. Again and again, the Chinaman teases No Name. Then he opens his hand, and No Name plucks the jerky.

I walk toward them.

"Sugar," Mister Beale yells. I pretend I don't hear.

Missus Beale screeches; Mister Waters hollers. All the River Road folks are shouting at me to come back.

The Chinamen shout back words I don't understand. I hope they're saying, "Welcome." "Let her visit." "She's a wonderful girl."

I keep walking.

Missus Thornton booms, "Misbehaving, disobedient child."

I don't look back. I keep focused on the Chinaman

and No Name. Both of them are calling me without saying a word.

I...am...almost...there.

"Sugar!" Mister Beale scoops me up like a sack. I can't get down, get away.

"Knee-how," I shout.

"*Ni hao*," the Chinamen answer back. Even No Name seems to dip his head, bow. The young Chinaman holds him close.

Mister Beale sets me down on the porch. Missus Beale clasps my hand, tight.

I sigh. *Next time*, I promise myself, *I'll make it all the way across the yard.*

Planting Day

Planting Day is the start of cane season. But there's never been a Planting Day with China-men. Too bad River Road folks and China-men stand separate in the field. Makes no sense. We're getting ready to do the same work!

All day until sunset, men will cut sugar stalks into pieces. A bud needs to be growing on each piece. All day until sunset, the rest of us will dig, dig, dig, row upon row, lying cane flat, and covering it with dirt.

Billy walks beside his pa and Tom, the Overseer. He looks happy. No studies for him.

I'm a worker. Me and Billy were never pirate captains.

Mister Wills clears his throat. He looks like a squished bear, all stomach with a little head. His voice booms, "Mister Tom will make sure none of you cheat me of an honest wage.

"River Road folks know what I expect. Chinamen, you may have worked for the British in Guiana. But this here is Louisiana. Nowhere is as tough as here."

Mister Tom grunts, agreeing.

"Mornings, Billy will be learning cane." His pa grips his shoulder.

Surprised, River Road folks murmur.

I feel terrible. Billy's going to be a boss and do nothing. Just like his pa. I'll be working.

Weee-aaa.

A bird soars, its wings wide, fluttering against the blue sky. An eagle? When his beady eyes look down, I bet all he sees are specks. Specks of people stuck to dirt.

Mister Tom cracks the whip.

I put on my straw hat. The Chinamen have better ones—with wider brims and pointy tops.

Two Chinamen start cutting. Their silver blades slicing, buzzing through cane.

The rest of us make furrows.

Some, like me, use hoes to bury the cane.

Though the morning is chilly, sweat layers my neck and back, drips from my forehead, down and off my nose. Not working, my body got soft. Now my neck and shoulders are on fire.

I try to work as hard as the Chinamen, but I can't keep up.

Mister Petey can't keep up.

Mister Beale can't keep up.

Mister Wills is smiling, happy, slapping the Overseer's arm. "I told you. This is the future. Plenty of workers. Strong, hardworking men."

The Overseer frowns, stubborn like a mule.

River Road folks grumble. Softly, so Mister Wills won't hear.

Billy proudly walks behind his pa.

The Chinamen just keep working as the sun fries our backs.

Missus Beale huffs and puffs. Mister Beale grunts. Mister Petey sweats like rain. Even Missus Thornton is working as hard as she can. Rubbing his lower back, Reverend Thornton gulps water.

Chinamen say nothing. Just keep working. They start on a new row. Moving twice as fast as the old folks. They move calmly, their pointy hats and high-collared shirts bobbing, fluttering up, down, and forward. Cutting stalks, digging dirt, and burying cane. Row upon row. It'll take a month to plant all the cane that needs to grow.

I remember Missus Beale saying, "We may all lose our jobs. Our homes, too." That's why everyone is working so hard! Acting like today is the last day of harvest instead of the first day of planting. Maybe Mister Wills thinks he should only hire Chinamen?

I think: *River Road folks need me.* But how can I help? Usually when work is hard, we sing, "Hoe, Emma, Hoe."

Today is new. The Chinamen are new. Maybe we need a new work song.

I clear my throat and sing:

> *Cane needs planting. Dig it deep.*
> *Grow, cane, grow. All day, all night.*
> *Hey, yah. Hey, yah.*
> *Cane-planting gal. I'm a sugarcane gal.*

Mister Beale, head tilted, looks at me, quizzical.

I almost stop singing. But I raise my head, downswipe the hoe, singing louder.

Reverend yells, "Bless you."

Mister Petey hoots, "Go on, girl!"

My spirit lifts. River Road folks are proud of me.

Missus Beale adds her soprano; Mister Beale, his bass. Miss Thornton sings off-key, but everyone, except the Chinamen, sings my made-up song:

> *Cane needs planting. Dig it deep.*
> *Grow, cane, grow. All day, all night.*

Hey, yah. Hey, yah.
Cane-planting gal. I'm a sugarcane gal.

Even the men say *gal*, and I'm so happy.

Bodies are moving faster, plucking, burying, stomping down cane.

The Chinamen keep working.

My hat bobs as I bend and stand, bend and stand. I'm almost shouting my song.

The "hello" Chinaman, a row across and in front of me, stops, watches, listens to my voice. I sing to him, my voice strong. But pleading, too. I'm trying to make him hear, understand the worries of River Road folks.

He slowly smiles. I think he feels the rhythm of the song. Then he bows.

I bow back.

He whispers something to the Chinaman beside him, who whispers to the next and the next.

Then, amazingly, they all slow down. Not a lot. Just a bit. The cutters slow first. Then the rest, digging, planting, bending up and down, hoeing earth, slow down, too.

We River Road folks catch up, looking like a long rope. Straw hats, bobbing. Digging rows, planting stalks. Africans and Chinamen, working in time; us, singing. All of us moving, in the same rhythm—steady, strong.

I start cutting, singing again.

Mister Wills and the Overseer scratch their heads. They're watching but aren't seeing clear. River Road folks don't really see, either. They just keep worrying, working.

They don't know the Chinamen are kind.

糖

Everyone hurts.

I wish I could slip off my sore body like a shift. But old folks are worse; some don't eat, just go to their shacks, lie down, and sleep; others rock on porches, grunting, moaning, "Can't trust Wills. Can't trust Chinamen. Can't trust nobody."

I sit on the porch with Reverend, Mister Beale, and Mister Petey. (Missus Beale is sleeping.) Across the yard, we watch Chinamen eat warm rice from bowls.

We're too tired to cook—eat cold leftovers. I gulp meal cakes.

"Next season, we won't have jobs," says Mister Petey. "Use me up as a slave, replace me when I'm old."

"That's what Wills wants." Mister Waters nods.

"Chinamen, too," growls Mister Petey.

"I think the Chinamen are nice."

"I won't have it, Sugar. I won't have you near them," scowls Mister Beale. "I won't."

"You're not my pa."

"What?"

"You're not my pa," I say, louder. "How come I can't decide who I can see? How come I can't decide my friends?"

"We don't trust these men, Sugar."

"I like Chinamen. Reverend, don't you preach 'Treat folks like you want to be treated'?"

"Well, now," says Reverend, not looking at me, twiddling his thumbs.

"Sugar," says Mister Beale, "folks get along best with folks like them. Always been that way."

"Seems cowardly."

"Not cowardly." Mister Beale stoops. "Careful. Safe. We don't know these men, Sugar." His brows crinkle.

My head shakes before I speak. Mister Beale's forgotten how it feels being young. "Didn't you tell me to keep my spunk? Didn't you?"

"I did."

"Me and Billy keep separate. 'Cause he's from the big house. But the Chinamen are here. In our yard. Not right to keep separate from everybody."

Mister Petey glares. Reverend murmurs prayers.

"Caution never hurt nobody."

I almost ask, *Did caution keep you from going north?*

I clutch Mister Beale's big brown hands. "If you were a boy, not old ... if you were young again, what would you do?"

Mister Beale's eyes glower, pushing out the day's light. His face is tight, twisted. Then he sighs; his wrinkles smooth.

His fingers squeeze mine. "If I were a boy, nothing could keep me away from Chinamen."

"You're going to let her go?" asks Reverend.

"I don't think Chinamen are a match for Sugar," answers Mister Beale.

I hug him, then run across the yard, scuffing dirt,

letting my shawl flap and fly. "Knee-how. Knee-how."

I run up to my first "Knee-how" friend. His forehead is broad; his silk hair blacker than the night. His hands are tucked inside his sleeves. His eyes, half moons, see me, making me feel special. Up close, I know I didn't make a mistake. *In the field, he understood me. He made his friends understand me, too.*

"Thank you," I say, breathless. "You understood my song."

He bows. *"Xie xie."*

" 'Sheh-sheh.' You're saying 'thank you,' too?" I feel proud learning new words.

"Yes. You sing good."

"You speak English. What's your name?"

"Bo."

"Oh, Beau," I say. One of the sugar merchants is named Beauregard! Terrible name, and Mister Beauregard knew it, too. He said to Mister Wills, 'Just call me Beau.' *Poor Chinaman, he must be a Beauregard, I* think, but don't say. I'm trying hard for better manners.

Beau leans forward and with a stick, scratches in the dirt:

" 'Bo,' my name."

Chinamen are talking softly, darning clothes, or smoking pipes.

Beau writes again:

柳公

"Liu—that says 'Master Liu.'" He points to a man watching us from a porch rocker. Others, sitting on the steps, watch us, too. "Your name?"

I wish I could make up a new name. "Sugar," I say softly.

"Sugar. Yes, we work hard. Picking sugar."

"No. I'm Sugar."

"Cane?"

"No, Sugar. Just plain Sugar. That's my name."

Master Liu says something. The men laugh. I think they're making fun of me.

Beau scratches:

"Your name in Chinese. Can't write English." Beau shrugs sadly.

It looks beautiful—a tiny picture; a perfect sign.

I squat, my fingers floating above the blocks, the overlapping lines. Even in the dirt, the markings look pretty. Seeing my name is magic.

"Master Liu says *Sugar* means 'very sweet.' A nice name for nice girl."

"Why you call him *master*? Aren't you free?"

"He's our elder. Knows many things. Led us here. He's teacher. We honor."

"Master Liu is like Mister Beale. He teaches me."

"*Master*. Sign of respect. Just like bow." He bows. "For respect."

I look at Master Liu. He's smiling, rocking back and forth. I like his kind of master.

No Name, his black coat glistening, rubs against Beau's leg. Master Liu speaks, in Chinese, his voice floating high and low.

Beau looks at me. "Master Liu says you're strong, too. Says you must be born Year of Monkey."

"What's the Year of the Monkey?"

"1860. Ten years ago."

"I'm ten!"

"Master Liu is wise."

"Metal Monkey," says Master Liu.

He speaks English, too.

"Metal Monkey," says Master Liu, "is fighting monkey. Great spirit. Strong."

Master Liu speaks more Chinese. Beau grins; the other men chuckle.

My feet start twitching. I think they're making fun of me again.

"Master Liu asks, 'How many languages you speak?'"

I think, *Just one.*

Beau tilts his head. He's watching me, his black eyes twinkling, looking deep inside me.

My palms are sweating. Beau looks like Ma did, encouraging me. Like when she expected me to remember something, to know something that I didn't think I knew. "*Think, Sugar,*" she'd say.

"Two languages. 'Sheh-sheh,' 'thank you,'" I say proudly.

"Very smart girl," says Beau.

"Sheh-sheh, Mister Beau."

"Just Beau. I'm youngest. Student."

I like his face, round like the moon, and glowing like it, too. His eyes have spark.

I decide to be even bolder. "Friends?" I ask, stretching out my hand, all scratched and pricked from cane.

Beau stares at my hand. I'm scared he won't take it. Maybe he doesn't know about shaking hands, only bowing.

I want to pull my hand back—it's ugly, dirt beneath

my nails, sticky cane on my thumb—and stuff it behind my back.

Beau, his rough hand swallowing mine, grips and shakes.

"First American friend," he says.

I say, "First Chinaman friend."

"Chinese. Chinese friend."

"Chinese."

Master Liu joins us, his arms crossed, his hands inside his sleeves. Smiling wrinkles etch the edges of his eyes, his mouth.

Master Liu's not nearly as tall as Mister Beale, but he looks at me like Mister Beale does. Like I'm important.

"You, Mister Beale's daughter?"

"No. But I try to do what he says."

Across the yard, Mister Beale, Reverend, and Mister Petey are watching me like hawks.

"You loyal." Master Liu nods. "Metal monkeys always loyal."

"Do they get into trouble? I get into trouble all the time."

"Monkeys have energy. Many ideas."

That's me, I think.

No Name brushes against Beau, and he picks him up. "Cat's name?"

"No Name."

"His name?"

"No Name. I mean, he doesn't have a name."

"So sad," says Beau. "Just like Cat in Chinese calendar."

"When one is born," adds Master Liu, "depending upon year, you become connected to animal. Rat. Horse. Pig. Or Monkey, like you. You also become connected to elements. Like Wind, Earth, Water, Metal. You're Metal Monkey. Strong, you won't break."

I puff my chest.

Master Liu says softly, "Cat, so sad." He scratches No Name. "Long time ago, Emperor Jade, great Emperor of Heaven, called all animals, 'Tomorrow, I assign a special year to each of you.'

"Cat was so excited, he told Rat. 'Promise, friend Rat, tomorrow we will go together.'

"But next morning, Rat didn't wake Cat. Rat tricked Ox to let him ride on his back. With Ox's strong legs, they got to Emperor very fast. Quick, Rat jumped off Ox's back, landed at Emperor's feet.

"So, in calendar, Year of the Rat, first. No Year of the Cat. Forever and ever, Cat hunts Rat. Enemies."

Everything inside me is tingling. All my tiredness is gone.

Beau's eyes are sparkling; he's rubbing No Name's neck. No Name is purring.

"You told me a story."

"Chinese tale."

"About animals. Like Mister Beale. Like Br'er Rabbit and Hyena."

Beau stoops before me. "Master Liu tells stories all the time. Here," he says, pouring No Name, black legs and white tummy, into my arms. "You should name."

No Name's head bobs, his green eyes look at me. I never knew No Name was so soft. Much softer than chickens. His tiny, pointy ears flick.

"Name?" Master Liu's voice sounds like flowing water. "You name?"

I think, quick. "Jade. Emperor Jade."

"Sugar!" hollers Mister Beale. "Time for bed."

Startled, Jade leaps and runs away.

I bow low. Master Liu bows, too.

I bow. Beau bows.

We all bow again.

Imagine. Chinese men telling me stories.

I want to say something special. But all I say is, "You have pigtails like me."

I walk back to my shack thinking about Rat, Cat, and Monkey.

Tricksters

River Road folks stand quiet in the field, smelling of lard, cayenne. Everyone's back, legs, and hands are aching. I ache, too. But I also feel like I can fly. Just lift my arms and rise. Or else float free down the Mississippi's muddy water. It's exciting meeting new people, making new friends.

Tom, the Overseer, hollers, "Work! Get to work!" He cracks his whip.

"Earn your pay," says Mister Wills.

Billy walks beside him. "Earn your pay," he echoes.

The Chinese form a line, facing the River Road

folks. Dark across from light. Off to the side, Mister Wills, white and ruddy, stands. Billy's much paler, and Mister Tom's sun-browned. Almost as brown as me.

I lift my hoe, then stop. Nobody's moving. River Road and Chinese folks stare at each other.

Reverend lifts his hand high. "Another trial. Slavery. War." Reverend is testifying, praying in the field! "Lord, we're grateful we're free. But our bodies are old. Give us strength."

"Stop this nonsense. Get to work," shouts Overseer Tom, snapping his whip, glancing nervously at Mister Wills.

Something's happening. River Road folks are talking to the Chinese with their bodies, not their mouths. All the grown folks are leaning forward, some with outstretched hands, some just still, their eyes questioning. Some, their hands clasped together, not pleading, but, instead, quietly asking, waiting.

Mister Wills and Billy are bewildered. Overseer Tom is sputtering like a lame rooster.

River Road folks look to Mister Beale, waiting for a signal, some sign. Mister Beale walks, stands right in front of Master Liu. He says, firm, "We all have to make a living. All God's children have to live."

Master Liu bows deeply. Mister Beale nods. The two men look so different but the same, I think. Both lead. One by one, Missus Beale, Mister Petey, Reverend and Missus Thornton, Missus Celeste... all the River Road folks walk and stand beside a Chinese man. I stand beside Beau.

Then, almost like a dance, we all start moving.

River Road folks are digging, planting cane. Working hard.

Chinese men are digging, covering cane. Keeping to our pace.

My body feels it first—everyone working in unison.

When the Chinese start to go faster, Master Liu says something only the Chinese can understand. Like pulling reins on horses carting cane, Master Liu is holding his men back. Keeping them from working faster.

Overseer Tom is scowling; he always scowls. Mister Wills is just happy.

The Chinese men won't make us lose our jobs. *I don't know how I know, but I know.* Master Liu's words are holding his men back. Not a lot, just some. It's like yesterday when I sang my work song. But now the grown folks are making sense. Figuring each other out.

Nothing to worry about, I think. Like Br'er Rabbit, grown folks are tricking Mister Wills and Overseer Tom. They're not being lazy, just making sure everyone—young and old, Chinese and African— work the same amount.

I think, *I'm special.* I can keep up with grown folks. I'm strong. Just hoe, dig, bend, plant, cover cane with dirt. Over and over and over 'til sunset.

৵৹

After planting, the Chinese go to their side of the yard; we go to ours. I'm thinking, *Grown folks are dumber than hyenas.*

Missus Beale pulls two cast-iron pans of corn bread from the hearth.

I say, "The Chinese probably think Manon and Annie are River Road's best cooks."

Missus Beale stiffens, her back ramrod straight.

"They don't know nobody makes corn bread better than you. Outside, all crispy brown. Inside, yellow, soft. *Dee*-licious!"

Missus Beale brushes the corn bread with cream.

"But the Chinese aren't really neighbors. I'm going to keep away. Not give them any of your corn bread."

Missus Beale peers at me. I smile sweetly, then I blurt, "See. I'm a good girl."

"No, you aren't," says Missus Beale, chuckling. "You just put me in the briar patch!

"Come on, Sugar. Grab one of these pans."

"Betsy, Manette, Marie," Missus Beale calls from the porch. "Can't have our neighbors thinking we can't cook."

Missus Ellie, Thornton, and Celeste fly in and out of their shacks.

"Better late than never," says Missus Beale, leading the way.

Missus Thornton carries a platter of sugary stuff. Missus Celeste brings pickled carrots. Missus Ellie makes the best red beans spiced with peppers. I hope the Chinese like fiery food.

"Don't drop the pan, Sugar."

The Chinese men are sitting in the yard on their shacks' steps. Master Liu sways in his rocker. When he sees us, he rises. The other Chinese stand, too. River Road folks come to a halt.

I look left, right. Nobody's smiling. Amazing. Grown folks don't know how to make friends!

"We brought food," I say. "Missus Beale makes the best corn bread."

Master Liu tastes the corn bread first. "Fine," he says. "Corn bread good as rice."

Missus Beale beams.

"Let's eat," says Mister Beale.

For the first time ever, everyone's on the same side of the yard.

*   *   *

Beau shows me how to make a rice ball.

I pop it in my mouth.

Over a kerosene flame, Beau stirs onions and greens. He scrapes into the round pan slices that look like brown bark. "Ginger. Good spice," he says.

Beau uses sticks to pick up food. "Chopsticks," he says. He hands me two.

I use one to stab the greens. *Splat.* Beau scoops them up before Missus Beale can see.

"Use your hands, Beau," I say when he tries to pick up corn bread with his sticks.

"Let's make corn bread balls." We make a dozen and pop them in our mouths.

Of all the Chinese, Mister Zheng seems the quietest and the scariest. There is a long, jagged scar over his left eye. It looks like a worm across his eyebrow.

I scoot beside him, watching him eat, watching his jaw and the worm scar jump.

"Mister Zheng, how'd you get that scar?"

"My brother threw rock."

He and I sit, cross-legged, side by side, eating

135

beans, greens, and onions, and corn bread. I think Mister Zheng looks like a pirate.

"I miss Billy."

"Billy?" asks Mister Zheng, his voice deep like a frog's. Not lilting like Master Liu's.

"Mister Wills's son. I'm not supposed to play with him."

Mister Zheng nods—slowly, up and down, up and down again, and he says something in Chinese.

I don't know what he's saying, but it sounds right, feels true.

Mister Zheng pulls a picture from his pocket. There's a tiny lady with two children—one on her lap, the other, almost as big as me, holding on to the chair. They're dressed like Mister Zheng, in black pants and jackets with high collars. They aren't smiling.

Mister Zheng smiles, proud.

Acting my most proper, I say, "Beautiful. Your family is beautiful."

"Is it too hot?" asks Missus Ellie, peering over shoulders. "In Louisiana, we like food spicy."

"Good." "Good." "Good food," say the Chinese, scooping spicy beans into their mouths.

I don't think Missus Ellie believes them.

"In Chengdu," says Beau, "very hot food."

Master Liu bows to Missus Ellie. She blushes. "We come from Sichuan Province. Famous for hot red peppers."

"That's where Master Liu found me," says Beau. "I cooked spicy food. Used plenty peppers. Will you teach me? Louisiana food?"

Missus Ellie is tickled, happier than I've ever seen her.

"Time for bed, Sugar," says Mister Beale. "Work tomorrow." Like a signal, all the River Road folks stand.

"Please, Mister Beale. A little longer. Master Liu knows stories like you. Good ones like Br'er Rabbit and Hyena."

"Well, now," says Mister Beale, encouraging everyone to sit again and gather close.

Master Liu speaks Chinese.

"What?" asks Mister Petey.

"The Changjiang river," translates Beau. "Waves behind, drive waves ahead."

Mister Beale scratches his head. "What's that mean?"

"Changjiang, longest river in China."

"Like the Mississippi in America," I add.

"Waves of the past help future," says Master Liu. "Like children. Each generation better than last."

"That's what my father taught me," says Mister Beale, shoulders back. "Each life builds upon the past."

"May I tell story, Master Liu?" asks Beau.

"Any animals in it?"

"Not this one, Sugar. Story, real life, true. Master Liu rescued me."

"From pirates?"

"No. From being poor. Being street boy. Mister Zheng, Mister Li, Chen, others, all farmers. All from Sichuan. Chinese clan.

"We sailed together."

"To pick sugar?" I squawk. "I can't believe it."

"Cutting sugar is better than starving in China," says Master Liu. All the Chinese men nod.

Lightning bugs blink. The fire is crackling, and the full moon is shining on our messy plates and leftovers.

Mister Beale hands Beau a long stick. "Show Sugar, please. Show her China."

Beau draws in the dirt. With his paw, Jade swipes at the stick.

"We come from China. To Guiana. Then New Orleans. See." Beau marks a spot.

The ground is telling a story.

"China." Beau points. "Shanghai. Port to the sea." He draws squiggly shapes to look like waves.

"Our home is Chengdu. Middle of China." His stick digs a hole in the middle of the dirt-shaped China.

I stare at the markings. China is huge. Like a giant kidney bean.

"China, big." Beau's arms are wide, and the stick makes his reach wider.

I squint. My mind can see a thousand men in Chengdu looking just like Beau.

"You came across the sea? Like Africans?" asks Reverend. "How long?"

Beau's eyes close, like he's unhappy, remembering. "Months. Bad," he says. "Very, very bad. Long journey."

"Mister Beale says Africans came to America chained, starving, and sick. Most weren't born here like me. Did folks die, Beau? Did they?"

Beau nods. "Some wanted to turn back. To go home. Back to China."

"Some did die," says Master Liu, looking straight at Mister Beale. "But we choose to come. Not captured."

Everybody's sad-eyed, mournful.

"Where's Chang...?"

"Changjiang?"

"Yes, where's Changjiang river?" Beau hands me the stick, then, his hand over mine, guides the stick. "Here, up to the Tibet mountains."

"That's where the river begins," I shout, excited. "North. Just like the Mississippi. The Mississippi starts north." *Me and Billy could raft down the Changjiang river in China.*

My heart swells.

I look at the Chinese. Gentle Beau. Master Liu with his kind eyes. Mister Zheng with his bullfrog voice.

I look at Mister Beale. Him and Missus Beale are holding hands, watching me.

"You're the wave, Sugar," says Mister Beale.

For the first time, I think it's fine to be new, to be young, not old.

I turn toward the Chinese.

I bow, slowly, 'cause I want to do it right. My hands press together like I'm praying, my head bends, reaching low, almost to the ground.

Master Liu says something I don't understand. Then, all the men, in unison, bow, ever so low, lower than ever before.

And I feel like warm water is washing over me. A deep, low bow must mean "more." Extra good, more respect.

"Work tomorrow," says Missus Beale, breaking the spell.

We all return to our shacks. I try to walk, not run.

Try to act dignified. But my feet barely touch the ground.

The world is **BIG**.

If Chinese men can come to Louisiana, I can go there—China. If African men can come to America, I can go there, too—Africa. The land where Br'er Rabbit and Hyena live! China—the land where Cat, Rat, and Ox live.

Inside my shack, I twirl like a leaf spun by cool wind.

Another Secret

I can't sleep. I'm so excited. I dream of places I can go. Shanghai. Chengdu. North, like Lizzie.

I don't mind my sweat-soaked sheet. I don't mind how stuffy my shack smells. Or the dirt in my hair and on my feet.

My money jar is open. I lay my dollars in a row. One. Two. Three. Four. Five. I wish dollars could breed like rabbits.

I hear a whistle. Billy!

Another whistle. Then another.

Billy's going to wake the Beales!

I tiptoe outside. Candles are snuffed, shacks are dark. I hear Mister Beale snoring (do Chinese snore?). Whip-poor-wills are screeching, eating bugs.

Another whistle. I run round back. "Shhh. I'll get in trouble."

Billy's freckles are bright red; the day's sun has turned his hair golden.

"Tell me about the Chinamen."

"Chinese. They're called Chinese. They like spicy beans. They don't like okra. Collards are okay."

"Oh," says Billy like I've said magic words.

"You better leave, Billy. I'm going to get in trouble."

"You like trouble."

"But the Beales don't. Your pa might run them off."

Billy stuffs his hands in his pockets. His whole body scrunches like a weight's pressing him down.

"You know it's true, Billy Wills."

"Not fair."

"Hush. You're going to wake the Beales."

"I'm sorry, Sugar. In the field, workers don't talk. I can only get to know them in the slave yard."

"Used-to-be-slave yard," I mutter.

"Ma's not sure the Chinamen are civilized."

"Chinese. Chinese men."

"Pa says, 'Lincoln ruined everything.'"

"I think President Lincoln did good."

"Pa says workers are scarce. Hard to get and keep. I told him that's why I should learn more about Chinese. I already learned not to say *Chinamen*."

"From me."

"That's why I'm here. It's not fair that you get to be with the Chinese and I don't. Not fair we can't play together."

I see stars, some blinking, some streaking across the sky. Mister Beale told a tale of slaves who decided to become blackbirds and fly back to Africa. Eagles are prettier, bigger.

I turn and climb an evergreen, hand over hand, foot over foot.

Billy rustles after me; it's like a race, but I win. Sitting on a branch, I raise my arms. "I wish I could fly!"

Billy's on a branch beneath me. We're both perched high.

"Look," says Billy, "the river, it's sparkling like

Ma's pearls. I don't have to fly; I can sail. Stars help you navigate. Go anywhere."

"I only know the Drinking Gourd. It points north."

"The Drinking Gourd is the Big Dipper. There're two dippers," says Billy, pointing. "A Big Dipper and a little one. See, Little Bear, Ursa Minor. The North Star is part of Bear's tail. Next to it is Ursa Major, the Big Bear. And there's Orion, the hunter. See his belt?"

"I see," I say, connecting dots in the sky.

"Just like there are paper maps for land, the stars are maps for oceans. I don't understand it all, but I'd like to."

"Me, too."

To my left, below, are the sugarcane fields, River Road shacks; to the north is the big house and the Mississippi. Up high, the stars.

I cling to the bark, liking how it scratches my arms and makes me feel strong. Billy scoots closer to me, clutching another branch.

"No secrets. Right, Sugar?"

I hold my breath, scared what Billy might say.

"One day I'm going to leave the plantation."

I'm shocked. River Road is going to be Billy's. Doesn't he want to keep it? If it were mine, would I stay?

I blurt, "One day I'm going to leave River Road, too."

"You should."

"Five years ago, I would've been a runaway."

"Yeah, Pa would've owned you."

"Then you would've. Right, Billy?"

"Naw. Anthony. If I'd tried to own you, you would've punched me."

"I would, too."

We're quiet, our legs dangling.

An owl hoots. Somewhere, there are eagles.

Billy pulls a kerchief from his pocket. He opens it, peeling back the cotton. Inside is a buttermilk muffin. My favorite.

Billy splits it in half, and we munch, crumbs dropping like flakes onto the ground.

I feel guilty. Billy should go. I promised the Beales to be good. But part of me wants to keep talking, be with Billy.

"Ever since I can remember, I've wanted to leave River Road," Billy says.

"See the world?"

"Yeah. Pa loves this place. I don't. Ma tells me to study. Be a gentleman. Pa says being a planter is good enough. 'Plenty hard work.'"

In a few hours, the sun will be a ball on the horizon. I'm going to be so tired.

"Billy," I say, glad I can't see his face. "There's something you don't know. It's so secret you don't even know you know it.

"I complain, but Missus Beale is right. I've got to work. You don't. Your pa can bring you the world. Snap his fingers and make Chinese appear. From all over the world, ships come to your pa's plantation to carry sugar to people I can't imagine. Like I couldn't imagine Chinese 'til I saw them."

I pause. "You don't ever work harvest. Everyone else works hard."

I look down. Billy's looking up, his jaws sharp, his lips stubborn. Evergreen shadows streak his face.

"Billy, can you write?"

"Sure, everybody can—"

"When Mister Beale tried, the Overseer whipped him."

Billy's head falls forward, his chin touching his chest. His shoulder blades are bony, tucked in. "You're saying I'm lucky, Sugar, and I don't even know it."

He looks up, giving me the "pity-pity" look, like Missus Thornton.

I smack the branch. "Don't you go feeling sorry for me. I won't stand it. I'm lucky, too. I've got Mister and Missus Beale, Br'er Rabbit and Hyena tales. I get to live with the Chinese. I'm a different lucky."

Billy is different from his ma and pa. Just like I'm different from River Road folks.

"I don't want to see you again, Billy Wills."

I hear his gasp. Relentless, I go on, scared I won't be able to finish.

"You don't know what it's like to work cane. You just walk and holler behind your daddy. You'll be just like your daddy, one day." My throat tightens. I can barely breathe. "Leave me alone. I don't like you anymore."

"You don't mean it. You don't."

"You're just dumb like a hyena. The Chinese are my friends. You've got it better than anyone I know. If you want friends, tell your pa to buy you some."

Billy doesn't move. I think he's trapped in the tree. I don't look down at him. If I look down, I know I'll cry.

Grown folks drew a line. Me and Billy crossed it. And now I've got to uncross it to keep the Beales safe. So they can keep making dollars.

"Sugar," Billy says softly. I can't help it, I look down.

Billy opens his pocketknife, scratches, carves S into the tree.

"S. Sugar, the first letter in your name is S."

Billy's trying to change the rules, teach me to write. But I can't risk hurting the Beales. "That's ugly," I say. "Looks like a snake. My name is prettier in Chinese. You've got to go, Billy Wills. We can't be friends."

Air stills; quiet feels loud.

Billy climbs down, his hands grasping branches,

bark, his feet finding toeholds. He inches down, down, down.

Billy's not as good a tree climber as me. I could slide down before he blinked. Rooster Ugly crows.

Billy lands on the dirt. He doesn't look up but runs faster than lightning. Faster than I've ever seen him. He doesn't look back.

My finger traces the S. I like how it curves. How the first letter in my name is etched forever in the bark.

Clang-clang.

The Overseer beats the triangle with a metal rod. *Clang-clang.* Time to get up. Cane time!

The worst time of day, and I've lost a friend.

Chinese New Year

It's Sunday. Reverend is getting ready to lead us in prayers.

Beating sticks together, Beau dances in the yard. "New Year. Happy New Year!"

"Beau," I say, "New Year's come and gone."

"It is Chinese New Year," Master Liu says, padding forward. "After your prayers, celebrate with us. We'll cook, play games. Tell stories. What do you say, Reverend? Mister Beale?"

"Sounds right fine," says Reverend. "Let's say prayers."

Missus Thornton whispers something into Reverend's ear. He clears his throat. "Master Liu, do you and your men pray?"

"Not to a god, like you. We honor ancestors. We seek harmony with good deeds. Some chant for human suffering to end."

"Just get rid of sugar," I murmur.

"Shhh," says Reverend. "A moment of silence."

Except Master Liu isn't silent. He chants quietly. I can't understand the words, but I feel my spirit lift.

The chant is like a song that never ends. It hums and buzzes, rising and falling, making a watery sound. It soothes. Like a lullaby, it opens memories in my mind.

I close my eyes.

I see Ma pretty, her hair, tied, inside a bandana, her arms reaching out for me.

ॐ

"Time to steam dumplings," says Mister Wang. Mister Wang has strong arms like Mister Waters. He and Mister Waters don't talk to each other much, but they play a game like checkers, with black and white stones. Mister Wang taught him how to play, and Mister Waters taught Mister Wang how to pluck banjo.

Over the community fire pit, there's a pot of boiling water. Each man holds a wide, round basket. They look like they're woven from sugarcane. "Bamboo," says Beau when I look at him, curious. Then, Beau shouts to everyone, "Shape dough into small circles. Like size of palm."

I make two circles.

Mister Zheng and Beau each carry a bowl. "Filling. Mine's spicy," says Beau. "Mine's sweet," says Mister Zheng.

Beau spoons his filling onto one of my circles. "Now fold it over and pinch the sides closed. See. First Chinese dumpling."

Mister Wang waves me forward. I lay my dumpling in his basket.

Soon, everyone is folding, pinching dough closed, laying perfect white dumplings side by side.

"Special coin in one dumpling," says Master Liu. "Whoever finds will be lucky all year."

Jade sits watching the baskets fill. Just as River Road folks like the Chinese, Jade does, too. He's friendlier. Like me, he was waiting for new people to make his life better. I stroke Jade's furry head.

"Now steam." Mister Wang places a plank across the boiling water pot. He puts the bamboo baskets on top of it.

"Master Liu, can you tell us a Chinese tale?" asks Mister Beale.

"I can, can't I, Master Liu?" I ask. "I know how Rat came first."

Master Liu nods.

"Emperor Jade had a race to see what animal years would come first—"

"On Chinese calendar," says Master Liu, encouraging.

"Cat told Rat, 'Let's go together.' But next day, Rat let Cat oversleep. Because Rat has tiny legs, he hitched a ride on Kind Ox. Just as Ox was about to cross the finish line, Rat hopped off and won. Year of the Rat."

Mister Beale chuckles. "Rat's tricky like Rabbit."

"What about the other animals?" asks Missus Ellie.

"Tiger swam strong across a river. He came in third. Then came Rabbit hop-hopping, floating on river logs. Rabbit's smart like Br'er Rabbit. Not big but smart. Master Liu, I forget who's next."

"Dragon," says Master Liu. "Dragon should've won, but he helped a village escape a flood. Even gave a push to Rabbit on his log. Dragon good, good soul.

"Snake hid in Horse's hoof. When Horse made it across the water, Snake squirmed out and scared it. Snake came in sixth. Horse, seventh.

"Ram, Monkey, and Rooster crossed together on raft."

"So that's eight, nine, and ten," says Reverend.

"Dog is eleven," I say. "Dog was busy playing. Running, jumping in water. Pig was last. His belly full, he'd taken a nap. Slept too long."

"Sugar, Monkey." Master Liu touches his chest. "I, Horse. Tell me," he asks, his hands sweeping wide, "when you were born?"

River Road folks start calling out the year they were born.

Mister Beale, like Master Liu, is a Horse. Mister

157

Petey is a Dog. Reverend was born in the Year of the Ox. Missus Thornton is a Rooster. I believe it!

Mister Aires, who's quiet and always stands to the side or sits in the back, pushes forward. "Master Liu, what if you don't know when you were born? What if you were born a slave and no one wrote it down?"

"Pick an animal who calls to you."

Thinking, Mister Aires looks serious. Like this is the most important question in the world. Then he says firmly, "Pig."

We laugh.

Beau hollers, "Dumplings cooked."

"Happy New Year." "Happy New Year," folks say, voices overlapping, stopping and starting, as buns, some sweet, some spicy, fill their mouths.

"Happy Chinese New Year."

Master Liu offers me a dumpling. I bite into it. No coin.

Then, Missus Thornton squeaks, shrill. "I won. I won."

"Good luck," says Master Liu. "All year, good luck."

"Can I see?" Missus Thornton shows me the coin. It has Chinese writing and a hole in the middle.

"It's pretty," I say, being nice.

Missus Thornton blinks, like she's not sure I'm me.

Jade flicks his fluffy tail, rustling dirt. River Road folks—African and Chinese—are resting, bellies full. Some are smoking cheroots; some, just talking; some, rocking on the porch, sitting on steps, or crouching before the community fire.

I pat-pat Jade's head. I blink back tears.

"Sugar, why so sad?"

"I'm not sad, Mister Beale." I hold Jade really close, burying my nose in his fur. He licks my hand.

I sniff. "I like the Chinese. I like Chinese New Year."

"What's wrong?" asks Master Liu.

"Her mother died New Year's Day," says Missus Beale.

"Not Chinese New Year."

"But today reminds you?"

I nod.

"Let's honor grave," says Master Liu.

"We'll say a prayer," says Reverend. "Would you like that, Sugar?"

"Yes, please. Can I bring Jade?"

"And I'll bring you." Beau lifts me and Jade. "You need to eat more food."

I kiss the top of Jade's head. He purrs.

I'm bouncing just a bit. Beau is like a calm horse, his legs striding strong.

I like being carried. Beau smells of ginger and smoke. Not sugar. I feel safe. Like I don't have to worry about anything. Not even my own two feet.

Up here, I can even look Master Liu straight in the eye. Mister Beale's too tall. I'm only level to his neck.

Up close, I see how smooth Beau's skin is, how his lashes don't curl up but point straight down, and how his head is shaved around his forehead before his hair is pulled into a pigtail.

"Cemetery this way," announces Reverend.

Everyone follows. Past our shacks, the field. We trudge on and on, the baby cane paying us no mind.

The ground is level; then it slopes. Beau turns sideways and slowly sidesteps down. He holds me and Jade close.

There's a narrow trail. No one's speaking. The only sound is feet crunching rock and dirt. Like soldiers on the road. There's less cane. The sickly sweet sugar smell fades.

We come to a clearing. Mounds of dirt are studded with wooden crosses.

"Bones," says Beau. "Spirits everywhere."

Rows aren't neat like sugarcane. The cemetery is haphazard, cluttered, full. Like folks took a shovel to wherever there was room.

Shadows of crosses crisscross, overlap one another. Three black willows stand guard over the sad piles. Willow branches with streams of gray moss are touching the ground, like dropping tears.

Beau sets me down. Jade leaps to the ground.

"Over two hundred graves," says Mister Beale. Though there are no names on the crosses, Mister Beale zigs among the graves, to the left and twenty graves back, and points. "My youngest son lies here."

I remember Ma's grave. It's far in the back. Two years old, her grave is the freshest.

Some of the grown folks are looking at me, "pity-pity" looks; some are praying; some, chanting. Mister Zheng is studying the cemetery like it's a strange land.

Silence is heavy. Like there's a thick blanket of quiet pushing down on the graves. There isn't any wind. No sound of rushing cane. Nothing. Like we're all standing at the world's end.

"Sugar's hard," I shout. "Hurts everything. Everyone."

Mister Beale stands beside me. "Sugar kills."

"Amen," says Reverend.

"That's the truth," says Missus Beale.

Reverend moans deep in his throat. Others start making the sound. A wailing clamped tight. No mouths move, but it's like sorrow, pain, and dying are rolled into one sound, trembling in their throats.

"During slavery," says Mister Beale, his voice loud like he's telling one of his stories, "sugarcane farmers bought the strongest, biggest, fiercest slaves.

"They weren't afraid of disobedience, rebellion. They knew with hard work, the lash, all their slaves would end up here." He paused, looking at the graves. "Sugar kills. Louisiana masters counted on it."

I smell grief, sharp like a knife. I slip my hand into Mister Beale's.

"I don't know why," he says, "we, those of us left, survived. I don't understand how I got old. How any of us got old. We were supposed to die."

"We honor Sugar's ancestor. Her mother," says Master Liu.

"Missus Sarah. My ma was Missus Sarah."

"We honor Missus Sarah, who brought Sugar into the world."

"Do. See. Feel." That's what Ma said before she closed her eyes. Before dying, she said another word. "Survive."

Chinese and River Road folks are mingling in the graveyard—stopping, talking, pointing at crosses. Old and new neighbors together.

I'm glad I'm alive.

Fever

I miss Billy. Miss rafting. Worse, Billy hates me.
I would if I were him.

Cross-legged, I empty out my money jar.
Money, unlike sugarcane, grows slow.

When I'm old enough, I'll buy passage on a river-
boat. Find a place where I can be friends with
everybody.

"Hey." Billy stands in the doorway.

I gape. "Hey."

Billy's face is damp, sweaty.

I don't know why he's here. Or what he wants.

Maybe he's trying to make trouble for me? Show me he can do what he wants, whenever he wants.

But I can't bring myself to tell him "go." He doesn't look well.

Billy shoves back his hair. Moist strands stick, flattening out his curls.

"I got a new harmonica. Want to hear me play?"

I shake my head. "No trouble for the Beales."

But Billy doesn't see or hear me. He grips the silver bar tight. Like the thin bar is holding him, keeping him upright.

He blows. A thin, wailing sound. It grows stronger and sounds sad and beautiful at the same time. It sounds like air is pushing loneliness out then back in, out and in. If he keeps playing, I'm going to cry.

The tune speeds up, and Billy's fingers are moving over holes and shifting the harmonica across his mouth. I want to jump up and dance, but I know I shouldn't.

"Oh! That was lovely!" I clap. Splotchy-red, Billy wraps his arm across his belly and bows.

There's a shadow behind Billy. Missus Beale!

"How do, Master Billy?"

Billy's eyes are glassy. Too bright. He looks in Missus Beale's direction, but his head is twitching, like he can't see.

"Your pa wouldn't like you being here."

Missus Beale is ever polite. But I can tell she's not happy.

"I don't want to go. I want to play with Pepper."

"Who?"

Billy points at me. Then he's babbling. "She doesn't like her name. Never did. Call her Pepper. Maybe Salt. Anything but Sugar. Ought to have a name she likes."

"Master Billy, I think you ought to go back to the big house."

"I want to play with Pepper."

Missus Beale gives me a look. *Don't you dare play with this boy. Do it and you'll regret it*, she seems to say without saying.

Miserable, I shift, foot to foot. I mumble.

"What?" says Missus Beale.

"Can't play. Have chores." My voice grows louder. "Your pa wouldn't like it."

Billy is redder than a beet. He licks his dry lips. "You think you're so special. All of you."

"Now, Master Billy—"

"Wait 'til the Chinamen come."

"They're already here. The Chinese," I say.

But Billy is talking quick, breathless. "When Chinamen come, Pa won't need any of you anymore." He sneers at me, as if to say *'Specially you,* then runs off.

I want to cry but don't.

I look at Missus Beale. "Billy's not himself. Not feeling well."

"Don't matter. His pa doesn't want him here." Missus Beale sighs. "Hard truth, Sugar. We may all still lose our jobs. Lose our homes."

Come evening, the Beales invite me to join them for community dinner.

I say politely, "No, thank you. I'll fix my own."

"You sure?" Mister Beale asks, using his kerchief to wipe his forehead.

"I'm sure."

I want to throw myself into Mister Beale's arms.

Feel his arm hugging me. I want to eat Missus Beale's fluffy corn bread.

I shake my head.

The fire cackles, making my hot shack hotter. There's an outside kitchen. During harvest, it's where Manon and Annie cook. Tonight, everyone is using it to have a good time.

I hear Missus Thornton screeching. I never caught a skunk, so I don't know why she's complaining.

I smell rabbit. My stomach rumbles. I bet Missus Ellie is grilling it. Mister Jean, gray beard, gray hair, probably caught the rabbit in a trap.

Grown-ups outside; me inside.

Sometimes I think the Beales think they're my grandparents. But they're not blood kin. Nobody knows my real blood. Ma and Pa were sold off from their families. Ended up with Mister Wills. "Not a bad master, but not a good one, either," Ma used to say.

I pour meal into the boiling water. It thickens fast. I add a sprig of rosemary.

I set out two bowls. Two wooden spoons.

I fill both bowls with gruel. Sitting cross-legged on the floor, I imagine seeing Ma. Brown eyes, soft hair, and a smile to melt butter.

"Do you have enough?" I ask. Ma is sitting on the dirt floor, wrapped in a quilt. She's been sick since harvest.

"Eat. Keep your strength." I lift a bowl and offer it to the air.

No hands reach for it. I set the bowl down. I peer at what I really can't see. Ma's woeful face.

"Why'd you name me Sugar?" I was always too afraid to ask.

Maybe Ma thought I'd soured things but didn't want to say. If she hadn't had me, she could've gone with Pa.

But the dead don't speak.

I remember Ma's voice, like bells, answering, when I asked about my name, "Who's my baby? My, oh, so pretty baby?"

"Me," I say out loud to the smoky room. "Me," I repeat. Sweat drips from my nose.

"Ma!" I shout.

I throw my bowl of gruel across the room. *Bam.* It hits the wall. I throw the second bowl. *Bam.* My gruel is terrible. Sticky, gummy. Now I'll have to clean the wood. Put fresh dirt on the floor. But I don't care. I feel better after throwing the bowls.

⁓

The cowbell is clanging! Like a metal rattlesnake.

I jump up. *Clang-clang-clang.* It isn't work time. It must be a fire.

Let the cane burn, I think. *Burn-burn-burn.* But a wildfire can destroy our homes. Explode the refinery, spraying melted sugar. Burn a person from the outside in.

The bell clangs: *Help-help-help.*

I run outside, and everyone else is running wild, heading toward the plantation house and the calling bell. There's no smell of fire. Cane is swaying with the breeze. Moonlight makes the plantation house glow whiter.

Mister Wills is on the porch, ringing the bell. His shirt is open. His hair mussed. He shouts, "Jem. Send for the doctor. Billy's ill."

This is worse than any fire. I yell "Bill-ly," and dash up the porch.

Mister Wills catches me, lifting me off the ground. "No time for your mischief," he growls.

Missus Beale screams, "Sugar! Come back here."

I twist, squirm. "Billy needs me."

Missus Beale catches my hand and pulls. Mister Wills lets go. I fall on my knees. Missus Beale jerks me up.

"Jem? Doctor."

"He's off," answers Mister Petey.

"I've got to see Billy."

"Eugenie," says Mister Wills, "get Sugar out of here or I'll have Tom take her off."

"Sugar, you've got no friends in there," says Missus Beale, shaking me. "Stay out of the big house."

I feel like sugar, ready to boil over. Billy might die like Ma.

I run onto the porch. Manon blocks me.

"Let me in."

"That's enough, Sugar," says Mister Wills. "Tomorrow, I'll have you gone." His eyes are watery, sad. I think, *Mister Wills doesn't mean what he says.* He's scared, same as me. He doesn't want to lose Billy. Same as me.

I've tried hard to be good. Tried not to bring the Beales trouble.

My heart almost stops. What kind of friend would I be if I didn't help Billy?

"I'll go," I say in my best pitiful, Br'er Rabbit voice. Head bowed, I shuffle down the steps. Missus Beale drops my hand. Manon unblocks the door. Mister Wills heads inside. I see my chance.

"Billy," I scream, running as fast as Br'er Rabbit. "I'm coming."

I push pass Missus Beale. Her hands grip air. I dodge Manon. She yanks my pigtail. *"Yeeowww."*

"Sugar!" Mister Wills chases me.

I sweep past him on the stairs.

I reach the bedroom. Billy's thrashing on the bed, his face pale, his hair slicked by sweat. His bed is high off the floor on sticks! I inch closer.

"You shouldn't be here." Missus Wills looks crazed, her hair falling out of her cap, onto her shoulders.

Billy moans. Eyes dull, staring at nothing, Billy looks out of his mind. He's twisting, turning, tangling sheets. He looks like he's going to disappear in the big white bed.

Missus Wills whimpers, rocking her body back and forth.

I'm trembling scared.

Mister Wills arrives behind me and grips the bedpost like he's afraid of falling. "Sugar, get out of here!"

For the hundredth time, I don't do what Mister Wills says. I reach for Billy's hand; he clutches mine.

His hair soaked, looking dark brown rather than golden, Billy smells sour. Smells like Ma did before she died.

"Don't die, Billy. Please."

His chest rises and falls. He makes a horrible, gagging sound.

"You've got to get better. Please, Billy."

"Sugar, you don't belong here," whispers Missus Wills.

"Billy," I say, desperate.

"Sugar," Billy sighs. He twitches, drools.

174

"Sugar, get out of here!" Mister Wills grips my arm.

I squirm. "Let me go! I have to stay with Billy."

"Sugar!" screams Billy. He's sitting upright, eyes staring at nothing. His nightgown is soaked.

"Billy, I've been practicing my whistle."

I whistle.

Billy turns his head toward me, his eyes horribly dark. I *whoosh*, whistle bad.

Billy falls back on his side, his legs curled.

"Get out," says Mister Wills.

"Stay," begs Billy.

"I can help. Honest, Mister Wills." I turn to Missus Wills. She looks frightful. "I took care of Ma. I can help. Billy's my friend. Honest, Missus Wills."

Missus Wills studies me like I'm a new person. She touches Billy's hand, where his hand covers mine.

"Get out, Sugar," Mister Wills repeats.

"No, Pa." Billy bucks forward and back. "Stay," he wails. Sheets slide, crumble to the floor. "Stay." Our arms jerk up, down. It feels like Billy's crushing my hand.

175

With my other hand, I pat Billy, trying to steady him.

Face wet, Missus Wills tucks in sheets. "Whistle, Sugar," she says fiercely. "Whistle."

I whistle. Billy calms like a baby chick, his head cushioned by the pillow.

"Sugar stays," insists Missus Wills. Mister Wills nods.

Billy taught me to whistle. My sound grows louder. Clear.

ॐ

I sleep on the floor, next to Billy's bed. I've a pillow and a blanket; I'm more comfortable than I've ever been.

Billy's in pain. He won't eat. When he's awake, his mind is far from River Road. It's like he's in a dark field and can't find his way home. When he's asleep, he mutters, "Pirates. Snakes." He even calls out "Anthony." He asks for his ma and pa. He asks for me.

176

Doctor says the longer the fever lasts, the worse it'll be. "You have to ride it out. Pray."

All night, Missus Wills weeps "Billy, Billy, Billy" and holds his hand. I put cool, damp rags on Billy's head. When he's real bad, flailing, groaning, I whistle.

After three days, two nights, Billy's eyes open. "You whistle terrible, Sugar."

"I know it."

Missus Wills starts crying.

I put another wet rag on Billy's head. He lets it stay, then falls back asleep.

I feel ten feet tall, like I helped Billy open his eyes.

Every day, Billy gets stronger. He sips broth and sits with two pillows behind his back.

"What'd I have, Sugar? Yellow fever?"

"Nope. Doctor says you had some kind of brain fever."

Billy looks grim.

"Can't be right," I say.

"Why?"

"You don't have any brains."

Billy laughs. "That's a good one." Then he starts coughing. Missus Wills scowls as if Billy's coughing is my fault.

I sit in the corner, watching her feed Billy.

"Me and Sugar are going to play checkers."

"I think it's time for Sugar to go back to the slave quarters."

"Aren't any slaves," says Billy, broth dripping from his chin.

"Well, yes, that's true—"

"So, Sugar stays!" says Billy.

Missus Wills looks at Billy, looks at me, looks at Billy, then looks at me again. Her face is pinched like she's eaten a sour pickle.

"At least until I'm better, Mother." Billy smiles like I think angels might.

Missus Wills's spoon clangs against the bowl. "Sugar, you can stay." Then she says stiffly, "You've een a help."

Billy winks.

I curtsy with the biggest smile.

⁎

I never knew being sick could be fun. When I'm sick, Missus Beale brings me a muffin and a cup of water. She tells me, "Sleep," shutting the shack door to keep out the light. If it's harvest time, sick or not, I work.

When we were slaves, the Overseer smacked his whip against any sick person's back. He'd say, "The lash is the best medicine." He never struck me; I was too little.

But now if we're sick, we lose pay. If we don't get pay, we can't pay rent, and I can't add money to my jar.

I'd be sick all the time if someone fed me, rubbed my head, and tucked soft blankets beneath my neck.

Billy's room is filled with light, and his bed has three quilts.

Six people could live here! It has everything. Toys.

A table, chairs. Even an old rocking horse Billy's grown too big to rock. He's got a shelf filled with river stones. Another shelf filled with books.

Billy's fiddle leans against the wall; on the floor lie sticks and a snare drum.

Billy teaches me the harmonica.

I blow. *Squeal. Squeal. Squeal.*

"Spare your breath, Sugar. Don't rush it."

I blow again.

"Nice and gentle."

Mmmm. Mmmm. Mmmm.

I get better.

I blow the harmonica. Billy bangs his drum. Missus Wills leaves, her hands covering her ears.

Sometimes, me and Billy play checkers. I always pick black, Billy, red. Because he's sick, I let Billy win. Sometimes.

When Billy naps, I open his books, but most of the markings mean nothing to me. I play with his tiny Confederate soldiers that lost the war, touch his instruments, amazed how Billy can make them come

Mostly, I stand at Billy's window. (Mister Wills got it fixed.) I open the glass, and warm air sweeps over me. A magnolia tree blooms outside.

Beyond the tree, I see the river. It's the most beautiful sight. I can see sailboats, steamboats, and rafts. Pelicans dive, pluck fish from the water.

Looking south, I can see where the river meets the sky. I wish I could swim, sail, or fly to that spot and beyond. I wish I had Billy's window.

Outside my door, cane stalks taunt me.

From Billy's window, I feel hope. Believe, one day, I'll be able to go wherever I want.

༄

Billy sits, his bare skinny legs pink. His nightshirt is blue, as light as his eyes. He runs his hand through his hair. "You're a good friend, Sugar."

"I know," I answer, grinning.

He reaches in the nightstand drawer. "For you."

The Chinese finger trap.

"Oooooh," I say. Red and yellow threads, braided, sparkle and glow. Everything about the finger trap is special—where it came from, who made it, how it works. Nothing about it is from me and Billy's world.

"I can't take this."

"Why not?"

I can't say in words. I twirl the finger trap. The colors blend like sunset. I don't have anything to give back.

"Didn't we swear friends?"

"We did."

Billy's different from me. So how'd he know of all the things to give me, I'd like the finger trap best?

Tomorrow, I'm going home.

But my shack will look different now that I've lived in the big house. Bare, unpainted, no rug, no bed, not even a chair to sit on. I got used to seeing my face in Billy's mirror. Until now, I didn't know there were such things to miss.

Not far from the big house, my home is a different world. But I'll be glad to be with the Beales, glad to ¡oo Rooster Ugly from pecking at the chicks. Glad ¡arden again.

But the real difference is that I'm going back to the fields.

"Did I ever tell you about Br'er Rabbit?"

Billy shakes his head.

"Billy Wills, I'm going to give you something you don't have. A Br'er Rabbit tale."

"Is there a hyena?"

"Listen and see." I climb atop a chair. "Well"—my voice squeaks, so I lower it—"every year, all the animals need to help with gardens. Else all the animals won't have any food."

"Animals don't garden."

"Hush, Billy. It's a tale. All kinds of wonderful things happen in tales! Now, where was I? Oh, much as I love Br'er Rabbit, he's lazy."

"Like me," says Billy, hopping up, jumping on his bed. "I've been lazy all week."

Your whole life, I almost say. "Billy Wills, are you going to pay attention or not?"

Billy plops down; pillows and a quilt bounce off

the bed. Hands clasped, Billy's trying not to laugh. A gurgle pops out like a burp!

"Billy Wills!" I wag my finger like Missus Beale.

"Lion was planting peas. Rooster was pecking corn, layering it in the dirt. Hen liked"—here I shivered—"okra. Beaver only wanted watermelon. At harvest, he'd whack it open with his tail.

"Hyena, who liked eating Rabbit, Chicken, and Squirrel, was plowing new rows with his nose. He'd stick his nose in the dirt, deep, then trot, earth clogging up his nose. He'd sneeze at each row's end! He hated it. But the rule was: Everyone works, else you don't eat!"

"So, no eating nobody."

"That's right, Billy Wills. 'Cept Hyena was sneaky. Everyone knew Hyena, if he could, would eat them all. 'Specially Br'er Rabbit."

"Meat on the bones."

"That's right. Br'er Rabbit had a nice, fat tummy 'cause he was laziest. His job was to plant lettuce. Which isn't hard, if you ever planted lettuce. Which you haven't, Billy."

Billy grimaces.

"Br'er Rabbit complained, 'Too much sun.' He twitched his ears. 'Pesky, lazy flies.' He shouted at the crows. Of course, everybody shouted at the crows, with their sharp, flinty eyes. Crows refused to garden. They'd steal seeds quicker than a snap.

"Still, nobody liked a complainer.

"Lion roared, 'Br'er Rabbit, your complaining makes us tired.'

" 'Grumpy,' crowed Rooster.

" 'Frustrated,' said Squirrel.

" 'Now, now,' said Hen, like a chicken Missus Beale. 'We've all got to get along. No harvest, no food.'

"Hyena, with his thick pink tongue, licked dirt from his mouth and nose."

I jump off the chair. Billy leans forward, excited; I'm excited, too. Me and Billy have left River Road, left Louisiana; together, we're inside Mister Beale's African tale.

"Br'er Rabbit rasped, 'Water. I need water.' Before anybody could stop him, he hopped high, up into the bucket. And down, down, down he went, deeper into the well."

"Did he drown?"

"He should've. But rabbits are smarter than hyenas, squirrels, even bears."

"What happened next?"

"Rabbit liked the cool water. Tasty. He liked not having to work. But inside the well, it was cold, dark—"

"Wet."

"And he was stuck!"

"No way to climb out of the well."

"That's right, Billy Wills. Except...except there were two buckets."

"On a pulley." Billy grins, punches his pillow.

"Billy Wills, you're as smart as Br'er Rabbit.

"Rabbit started singing, 'Oh, the fish down here are fine. Fish. Fish,' he crooned. 'So many fish.'

"*Fish* was just enough to get Hyena's stomach rumbling. He peeked into the well. 'Fish, you say?'

"'They'll swim right into your mouth. Come on down.'

"Hyena was greedy. He jumped into the bucket and—*whoosh!*"

"*Whooosh*," says Billy.

"As Hyena flew down, Rabbit flew up."

"Like this." Billy stands, then—*boing, boing*—bounces on the bed.

"I'm Br'er Rabbit," I holler. "I'm free." Then—*boing, boing*—I fall on the bed.

Billy bounces, screaming, "I'm free."

"Goodness, what's going on here?"

Missus Wills.

Billy hoots. "Rabbit and Hyena." *Boing, boing.*

"*SUGAR*." Missus Wills's fists are on her hips.

I put mine on my hips, too. "*BILLY*."

Then me and Billy fall all over each other, tickling, kicking at the covers, and rolling with laughter.

"You two, stop it!"

We both sit. I know I'm in trouble, but it was worth it. Billy jabs me in the side. I jab him back.

"Stop it. Stop it."

Billy hits me with a pillow, and it bursts, sending feathers flying.

"*STOP IT AT ONCE!!!*" Missus Wills has never sounded so angry.

Little white feathers nestle in Billy's hair. A feather floats and settles on his nose.

"I'm sorry, Missus Wills." I've learned grown folks like to hear *sorry* when you're having fun.

Then Missus Wills's face twists funny. She blinks, triple-quick, clasps her hands, and starts to cry.

"Ma!" says Billy.

Oh, I'm in so much trouble! I scoot toward the door.

"I'm just so glad you're well," says Missus Wills, tears falling like spring rain. She hugs Billy, feathers and all.

"I started it," squeaks Billy. "Sugar—"

"Hush. It's all right. You're well. I was so frightened I'd lose you." She kisses Billy's face. All over. Nose. Forehead. Cheeks.

Billy blushes. "Ma, does this mean me and Sugar can play? Always?" he presses, his face sweet, his eyes wide, lashes batting, looking like one of them angels Reverend talks about.

Missus Wills pulls back, holding Billy at arm's length and looks at him, white, covered in white feathers; at me, black, covered in white feathers.

I hold my breath.

"When Sugar's not working, you can play."

III
Harvest
1871

Billy Cuts Cane

Through the summer, I could visit with Billy after working. He grew stronger.

This morning, Billy's joined us in the field again. Missus Wills shrieks like a hen chased by a fox. "Billy, you stop working this instant! Stop it. Mister Wills, stop him. He's not well."

"Ma, I'm fine." Billy's working beside me. He's wearing solid, good shoes; brown pants; and a white shirt with sleeves rolled up.

"Billy. This work isn't for you," shouts Mister Wills.

"How else am I going to learn about cane?"

It's late summer. The cane is ten feet high and for the next two months, we'll work hard to feed the mill's boiler. Each week our hours will get longer until, in the end, we'll be working with no days off, all day and through the night.

"Billy, owners don't work the field."

"Why not?"

"They just don't," blusters Mister Wills.

" 'Times are changing,' you said."

"Billy Wills," thunders Mister Wills.

River Road and Chinese folk are muttering, wondering who's going to win: Billy or his pa?

"Pa, I want to learn this."

"Are you sure, Billy?" I whisper.

"Sure."

First mistake: Billy touches the cane wrong, and his hand bleeds. At least ten pricks bubble red.

"It'll stop," I say. "Hold the cane near the base."

I know Billy's hurting, but he's not complaining.

"Billy, do as your ma says." But Mister Wills doesn't order "Stop."

Chinese and River Road folk keep working. Billy

does, too, like he can't hear his ma at all. He takes the machete and swings.

Second mistake: Billy's first chop isn't hard enough. He slices, hacks again and again. Finally, the cane breaks, and Billy grins, puts the piece in his bag.

I don't tell Billy there are hundreds more cuts to go. Rows upon rows.

I don't tell him how the cane will become hills. How we'll stop, stoop, and strain, and carry long stalks across our backs, and dump them into the wagon headed for the mill. Then start cutting cane all over again.

"Billy, I'm going to grab you out these fields this instant," says Missus Wills, her shawl falling to the ground, her hair escaping its pins.

All of us workers are watching Missus Wills, trying not to show we're watching.

Billy focuses on his sore hand, the cane and machete.

Missus Wills lifts her skirt, marching. Mister Wills grabs her. He whispers something. Missus Wills frowns, wraps her arms around herself, and stands, sweating unladylike in the hot sun.

The Overseer walks up and down the cane rows, checking everyone's work with his mean eyes.

Not even an hour and Billy's wincing, breathing hard. His face is beet red, his shirt, soaking wet.

Mister Beale gives Billy his hat. It sits low, in line with his brows.

"Thank you, Mister Beale," Billy says, his eyes barely visible.

"Pace yourself."

Billy nods. Side by side, we're bobbing up and down, hacking cane. Soon Billy's back is going to feel like a horse stepped on it. On his machete hand, blisters are popping.

I give him a cloth strip. "Wrap your hand, Billy."

"Thanks."

The rag will blunt some of the pain.

Mister Tom, the Overseer, snaps his whip, points his handle. He snarls so everybody can hear! "He's slowing the pace."

"That's my son," says Mister Wills, snarling right back, his fingers tucked tight into his belt.

"Billy won't last," mutters Mister Tom.

*   *   *

Billy lasts. He slows, though; we all slow. The heat and flies are horrible.

Billy wipes his face again and again. He rubs his sore hands on his pants. But he still cuts cane.

I smile, but he doesn't turn his head. He won't look at me.

"This work isn't meant for a child," shrieks Missus Wills.

"That's right," says Mister Tom. "Billy should go back to the classroom. We'll never make harvest with skinny Chinamen and old black grannies and grandpas."

"Tom, stop yakking," shouts Mister Wills.

"They're taking advantage, Mister Wills." The Overseer slaps his whip against his boot. "You can't expect me to bring in a good harvest. Not with lazy workers. Your boy, Billy, isn't helping." He towers like a scarecrow. "He's slowing the line."

"This is my plantation. Stop yakking, Tom, and do your job."

The Overseer stomps away to another row, hollering at Beau and Master Liu to work faster, harder.

Billy's face is hidden by the straw hat. He keeps working.

☙

Missus Wills goes inside the house; she's gone for a good while. She returns with Manon and Annie, marching down the wide porch steps.

It's not even lunch! Not even ten in the morning! Missus Wills and the cooks are carrying pitchers of water and lemonade. They've got platters of biscuits stuffed with smoked ham.

"Time for a break," says Missus Wills firmly. "Come on, come eat."

Amazing.

"Five minutes," shouts the Overseer. But nobody is listening to him. The Chinese men are bowing, the River Road men are taking off their hats, and the River Road women are curtsying, saying, "Thank you, Missus Wills."

Billy's dragging. I pull him by the hand and push him to the front. His ma gives him a glass of lemonade. His pa pats his back. Billy flinches, stretches his overworked back.

He takes a biscuit.

"Take another," says his ma.

"No, thank you. I'll wait 'til everyone else has one."

His ma sighs, pitiful. "I don't understand you, Billy."

"He takes after me," says Mister Wills. "Times are changing."

Missus Wills hands me a biscuit, a cup of lemonade. "Here you go, Sugar."

I feel the imp inside me. I know I'm supposed to keep my mouth shut. I know Missus Beale is going to be mad at me, but I can't help myself.

I look straight into Missus Wills's bright blue eyes and say, "I'm a child, too."

Nobody says nothin'. Nobody moves. Not Chinese men, not River Road folks, not even the Willses.

Finally, Mister Wills says, "Times aren't changing that much. Cane needs workers. Child or not."

"Biscuits. Lemonade," Overseer Tom grumbles. "Spoiling them. This'll come to no good end. You're spoiling these workers. I won't be responsible for it. I won't."

Mister Tom is truly upset, stomping, his whip dragging dirt. For the first time ever, I feel sorry for him.

"Mister Tom, I've got something special." He looks at me like I'm a bug. I reach in my shift's pocket. "Here," I say. "You can play with it."

"Sugar, don't—" yells Billy.

But Mister Tom has already taken the pretty red-and-yellow tube. The Chinese men are talking excitedly in Chinese, and then—

Mister Tom *howls*. "Get it off me! Get it off."

Mister Wills and the other grown-ups laugh while Billy shakes his head, covering his eyes. "Sugar, Sugar, Sugar."

Tom howls like a crazed hyena.

"Let me show you, Mister Tom. Let me show you how to get it off."

The Overseer growls, scowling, pulling like a bear, and still, the finger trap doesn't snap.

Everyone keeps laughing. Mister Tom slams the

tube over a machete's edge, slicing the finger trap in two!

Shredded twine unravels, falls to the ground.

I cry out, fall to my knees, trying to collect the strands. Red, yellow. Maybe it can be fixed? Woven back together?

A shadow, a flick of dust and dirt causes me to look up.

The Overseer's hand is high, the whip's stretching like an S ready to slash my back.

I scream, hands and knees tight, head down, protecting my face and arms.

Trembling, I know what's coming. I hear it— *swoosh*—but I don't feel it.

Instead, I feel a warm, heavy weight. Beau's body covers me. He flinches, shudders, deep.

"Get off my land," shouts Mister Wills. "Get off, Tom. Go!"

"You've gone soft, Wills. Yellow and black monkey men will ruin you."

"You'll be the ruin. I need cane workers. Willing workers."

Mister Beale helps me up; his hand on my back stills my trembling. Master Liu helps Beau.

"You've gotta keep a firm hand," says Tom, slapping his whip handle into his hand. "Else the white man stands no chance."

Mister Wills stands close, face-to-face. Mister Tom is bigger, but Mister Wills doesn't flinch.

"Don't come back, Tom. You don't work for me anymore."

Mister Tom is shocked. "I've been your Overseer for twenty years."

"You were a good one. But times have changed; you haven't."

Dazed, the Overseer looks at us workers. Like he can't believe seeing African and Chinese folks together. His face tightens as he looks at Billy, at me. I think, *He hates me.* Fierce, Overseer Tom steadies his stance. With his whip and fists, he looks like he'd fight us all.

"Wills, this isn't the last you'll hear from me. This doesn't end it."

"I'm not afraid of you, Tom."

But I am.

Beau's back drips with blood. Missus Beale and Master Liu care for him, cleaning his back, applying fatback and Chinese herbs.

Mister Beale keeps murmuring, "I couldn't move fast enough. Thank you, Beau. Thank you for getting to Sugar."

I pat Beau's hand. He winces as Missus Beale lays thin cotton on his back. "When you're better, I'll tell you a story."

"Now. Please. Better soon."

I exhale, happy the Beales and Master Liu are caring for Beau.

I tell them the funniest tale I know.

Kite Day

For two days, Billy doesn't cut cane. He's too sore.

Mister Wills says Billy's going to be Overseer. Mister Beale will teach him. I know Billy won't just stand, walk, and see. He'll work, cutting cane, making sure me and the women get help dumping stalks. He's already promised "lemonade and biscuits twice a day." Everybody's happier, working harder.

Even though it's harvest, Mister Wills has given us a last half-day Sunday.

I lie on my sack, staring at the ceiling. I'm bored. All the grown folks are resting. Even the Chinese are taking naps.

I stare at my walls, counting spiderwebs covering the cracks between logs. I could watch steamboats on the river. Maybe look for a skunk? Chase Rooster Ugly when he pecks at the hens? But I've done this all before.

Knock-knock.

"Sugar, Sugar."

I scramble up. "Who's there?"

"Beau."

I fling open the door. Sunbeams glow behind Beau. He's a shadow, but sparkling, dangling from his hand is a diamond-shaped cloth.

"Kite," Beau says. Light streams through the cloth; it's been dyed a bright red. Sticks are like bones behind the cloth.

"Tail," says Beau, stretching a string of white ribbons dangling and touching the ground.

Jade swats the ribbons. Beau rubs the cat's head.

"Good wind. Hurry." He turns, running, and me and Jade follow.

The kite drags in the dirt; still, Beau runs and runs, faster and faster toward the big house. Air catches the kite or the kite catches the air, I don't know which. The kite swoops up then down, bounces on the ground, then it's off...high, higher, it's tail wiggling like a captured snake.

I scream, "It's flying."

Beau stops, and the kite sails in the air, dipping and diving. *The cotton and sticks are alive*, I think. *Like a bird.*

Beau points. Billy's window. How'd Beau know this was the perfect place to go?

"Billy," I shout. "Billy Wills."

His head pops out the window.

"See." I point up at the clouds, the sun, the great blue sky.

Everyone quiets—even Mister and Missus Wills. The red kite is dancing, swirling and spiraling, and looking prettier than a flock of birds.

Beau hands me the rope. I hold it, feeling the push-pull of the kite and wind. It's tugging me, and I wonder if my feet will lift right off the ground and I'll fly, too.

"I'm coming down," shouts Billy.

"Come on," says Beau. "Fly the kite."

The kite bobs, and I can't help but think it's curtsying.

Everyone loves the kite. Me and Billy take turns, holding the ball of string, tethering the flying bird.

All the grown folks are awake! News has spread.

Chinese men are smiling, some smoking pipes, nodding. Mister Beale keeps slapping his thigh. Mister Petey murmurs, "Look at that. Just look." Even Missus Thornton is looking happier than she's ever been. Missus Ellie looks alert, not tired at all.

The Willses sit in rockers on their porch, smiling and holding hands.

I think this is the way River Road should always be.

Not speaking, me and Billy, heads upturned, steer the kite. Beau is standing a few feet behind us, in case we need him. Jade sits beside me. Ears twitching, he follows the red shape and ribbon tail.

⁂

"Seen a gator, Beau?"

"Gator? What's that?"

Me and Billy smile. "Let's go!" I hand Missus Thornton the kite's rope and she squeals with delight. Reverend is beside her, waiting for his chance to fly the kite.

Me, Billy, and Beau, hand in hand, take off running— past the cane fields, down to the Mississippi shore.

"Look, Beau." Billy skips a stone. The Mississippi shimmers. "Can you do that?"

Beau tries; all his stones fall flat and drown.

"Gators!" I shriek. We grab Beau's hand, and we're off running, kicking up water, hitting dry land. We run the shore's length to where the Mississippi narrows, shoots off, spreading like fingers, creating marsh.

"There!" I say.

Ten feet away are alligators—long, hard, sunning onshore. Two are so still they seem dead.

"One bite and you're gone."

"They can swallow you whole," adds Billy.

"Like dragon," whispers Beau.

"Hey," says Billy. "I've read about dragons. They're not from China!"

"Dragons, everywhere. Very special."

Beau sits on the grass, then leans backward until his back is flat. Me and Billy lie down on either side of him. The ground is cool.

"See, cloud," says Beau. "Stretch it out. Long. Give it a big head. Big teeth. Long tail. Imagine cloud breathes fire."

"I can see it," I say.

"Me, too. It's green."

"Why can't it be blue?"

"This dragon green," says Beau.

The three of us see the beast in the sky.

"It's a fat gator," I shout.

"Smart Sugar," says Beau, turning his head and smiling. "Dragon is like a fat gator."

"Are dragons real?"

"Yes," says Billy.

"If you want them to be," says Beau.

I sit and make bug eyes at Billy.

Frowning, Billy sits, too.

"I'll tell you dragon story."

Me and Billy both look down at Beau. He's lying, his arms crossed over his chest, his black shoes pointy in the air.

"You know dragon stories?" asks Billy.

"Yes. Many, many stories. But you must be quiet to hear."

Me and Billy grin. Beau has told us to hush. Me and Billy lie back, two small heads beside Beau's bigger one.

"Deep in waters of Chengdu—" starts Beau.

"Where's Chengdu?"

"Hush, Billy. It's China."

"Deep in waters lived Yellow Dragon. Skin gold like sun. Long neck with yellow eyes. Scales like huge fish.

"Yellow Dragon searched for a new home."

"I want a new home."

Beau turns his head. Half his face is squished flat by grass; the other half is smooth and round. "Good to search for better home."

"There's Yellow Dragon," I say, pointing at a cloud sailing past the sun.

Beau nods.

"Does Yellow Dragon eat anybody?"

"No."

"Too bad," says Billy.

Wisps of grass cling to Beau's hair. "Chinese dragons don't bite. They help people. Yellow Dragon helped Emperor."

"Emperor Jade?"

"Different Emperor."

"An Emperor is like a king. More powerful than a president," says Billy.

"Yes, most powerful." Beau's voice drops low. "Long ago, Emperor ruled great kingdom. Most kind, most giving to his people.

"They plucked rice from marsh. Like marsh, here, where gators live. Made good living."

"As good as sugarcane?"

"Yes, Billy. Maybe better."

I love Beau's voice. It's like cool lemonade. Like the Mississippi lapping against shore. Like a breeze making sugarcane dance.

"But three years in a row, the river where Yellow Dragon liked to sleep overflowed banks. Swallowing land, grass. Rising high, higher—"

"Like the Mississippi can."

"Rice paddies drown. Too much water. Everybody starve. Farmers hungry. Cows, pigs—"

"Chickens? Like Peanut?"

"Like Peanut. Chickens hungry. Everybody hungry. Emperor pray. Next morning, Yellow Dragon rises from river."

"What happens next, Beau?"

Beau sits, his ankles crossed. "Yellow Dragon promises to stop flooding. He flies high. Sees where the river starts. With his tail, digs channels. Miles and miles of channels.

"Dragon dares River. 'Flood, River. Try to flood.' And great River rises up. Snaps at Yellow Dragon."

Beau leaps to his feet.

Me and Billy stand, too. Beau raises his hands, his fingers curled like claws. He moves up and down like a wild wave.

"River rises. Water floods the channels. 'Ha,' says Yellow Dragon. 'Rice is safe.'

"River mad. Calls on storm clouds. 'Help me. Rain,' says River.

"Great storm. River rises and rises. River pulls back. Makes great wave, twenty feet high. Spits out water. Tons of water. But—"

"What?" asks Billy.

"None swallows paddies," shouts Beau, clapping his hands. "None makes it to Emperor's kingdom. The channels fill with water."

"Good," I holler.

"Wonderful," says Billy.

"Kingdom saved."

A huge cloud floats. I see Yellow Dragon, big, happy in the sky.

" 'Our home is your home,' says grateful Emperor. Yellow Dragon stayed. Made new home.

"Every year, villagers celebrate in dragon's honor."

*　*　*

Relaxing, we sit, our knees touching. Ants crawl over our shoes, our legs. None of us minds. The grass is soft.

"Beau, have you ever touched a baby gator?"

"No."

"Not as hard as grown-up gators," adds Billy. "Their skin is soft like velvet."

I don't know what *velvet* is—but I trust Billy.

"Like velvet," I say. "Really soft."

We sneak toward the gators sunning onshore. As we get closer, Billy points to the left, away from the water. "The nest will be in the bush." He points to the ground, and all three of us start crawling on our bellies.

There's a gator nest covered with sticks, weeds, but none of us moves.

Beau says, "Careful. Wait for father, mother to swim in water."

We wait and wait. And wait some more. We start falling asleep like gators.

Finally, Ma and Pa Gator, too hot, splash into the water. We three scoot forward and—there! Three baby gators.

Beau sighs like it's the most beautiful sight in the world. I pick up a baby and hand it to him. He holds it gently.

"So soft."

"Like velvet."

All three of us grin; then Ma Gator starts waddling up the bank. She can move fast as lightning if she wants. She doesn't see us yet!

Beau lays the baby in the nest.

"Tiptoe," says Billy. "Backward."

Don't turn your back on a gator! Not ever.

We three tiptoe over soft grass.

"Well, if it isn't monkeys. Yellow and black."

I spin. Beau turns slowly. It's Mister Tom, the fired Overseer.

"Pa told you never to come back," says Billy. "This is our land."

Mister Tom looks about to snap like a gator.

Beau holds himself still. So still he's lightly trembling. Beau's trembling makes me afraid.

Mister Tom carries a rifle; a squirrel's tail dangles from his sack.

"You shouldn't be hunting here," says Billy.

"Your pa stole a decent man's wage. He doesn't own me. I don't take orders from him." His face is sallow, sweaty-ugly. "Yellows and blacks ought to be owned. Your pa is an idiot fool."

"Don't you talk bad about my pa." Fists balled, Billy strikes out. Beau catches his collar. Beau's hand holds Billy while Billy's wriggle wildly. Beau's strong. He doesn't stop watching the Overseer.

"Let me go. Let me go."

"Quiet, Billy," I say.

"We go now," Beau says.

"Go back to where you came from. Your kind isn't wanted here. And you, Sugar," he sneers, "you deserve a lashing. Like your ma and pa."

I try to kick him.

Beau grabs me by my waist, lifting me off the ground.

"Billy Wills, you're no better. Spoiled and weak. You'll ruin River Road."

Beau is holding me and Billy both. Though we're twisting, fighting, Beau feels like a rock. He doesn't move. Alert, he keeps watching Mister Tom.

Mister Tom moves close, closer. He smells of tobacco and alcohol. He presses his face close to Beau's. Me and Billy stop struggling.

Beau sets me down, lets go of Billy's arm.

Mister Tom breathes heavy; Beau breathes steady, calm.

The Overseer is much bigger than Beau. Hair slicked back, brow damp, he seems desperate.

I see the shadow coming. I scream. The rifle butt hits Beau's head. Beau drops to his knees.

The gun points at Beau's chest.

"Get up, yellow man. Get up. I'd like to kill you."

Beau stands, blood trickling down the side of his face. The two men stare, Mister Tom intense, Beau confident like Yellow Dragon.

Billy hollers, "If my pa were here, he'd fight you. If my pa were here."

"Quiet, Billy. He isn't here," I say.

"Pa would teach him a lesson," Billy repeats stubbornly.

"Your pa won't teach me nothing," snarls Mister Tom, his thick face inches from Billy's. Billy steps back. "Your pa fired me. Replaced me with a child. Your pa's going to get what's coming to him. You wait.

"Yellow isn't better than white. Not ever. You hear that, Chinaman."

"Chinese," I say.

"Shut up."

Beau says simply—not too loud, not too soft—"We are leaving."

The muzzle rises. Right at Beau's heart.

"We leave," Beau says, clasping me and Billy's hands.

I imagine blood blooming on Beau's chest. A small circle getting bigger and bigger. Then, me next. Red flowing.

The barrel rakes against Beau's chest; Mister Tom is pushing hard, bruising skin. His finger twitches. All he has to do is pull the trigger.

Mister Tom wants to—*he wants to*—I know it—*he wants to*—he wants to pull, pull, snap the trigger.

Beau doesn't seem scared.

Mister Tom releases his finger, lowers the gun.

He's disappointed. I can tell. Like he wanted Beau to cry.

"Your time's coming," says Mister Tom, looking at Beau, then me. He moves backward into the brush, like we were snapping gators. The dead squirrel's head bounces, dried blood on his head, his beady eyes black.

"Why didn't you fight him? Why? Why didn't you?" Billy's asking Beau.

Beau keeps walking.

"My pa would've fought."

"He would've lost," I say.

"Still, he would've fought. Aw, Beau, how come you didn't fight?" Billy whines.

Beau keeps walking. I'm running behind.

Beau's disappointed Billy, just like Beau disappointed the Overseer. "Leave Beau alone, Billy. Leave him alone."

"I'm not talking to you, Sugar."

"Your pa wouldn't fight. He doesn't have to—he owns everything."

"What difference does that make?"

"Billy Wills, you're dumber than a rock."

Billy shoves me. I shove him back. Then me and Billy are fighting, rolling on the ground.

Beau pulls us apart. "No fighting. No fighting."

I cry, "If Beau fought and lost, what would've happened to us. To me?"

All the fear that'd been running deep inside moves through my body like syrup through cane.

The blood above Beau's eyes is clumpy, red-black.

"You were worried for Sugar?" sniffs Billy.

"Yes," says Beau. "And you, too. Wise men don't fight unequal battle. You lose before you have chance to win."

"Next time we'll invite a dragon."

"One that breathes fire," says Billy.

Family

I'm surrounded by my River Road family, Chinese and African. Misters Zheng and Petey play checkers; Mister Chin slices vegetables; across the yard, Reverend and Master Liu whittle fishing poles.

Missus Beale insists me and Beau snap beans. Sitting on the shack steps, we crack them. Jade, lying between us, purrs.

"Does it hurt?" I ask, pointing at the cut above Beau's eye.

"All fine."

"Mister Zheng's brother hit him with a rock. I wish I'd a brother."

"Why not me?" asks Beau.

"You?"

I snap beans. *Snap, snap, crack.* "Will your sister mind? Would she be my sister, too?"

Beau sets aside the bowl of beans. "My sister died. Just five. Long ago."

I slip my hand into Beau's. Even with the cut Beau looks kind, not mean, gentle, not harsh. I think, *Beau smells of cane like everyone else.* But he also smells of ginger.

Holding his hand makes me feel safe.

"Did your sister like to play?"

"Always. Didn't like sleep. Just play."

Beau puts Jade in my arms. I sigh. Jade is velvet.

"Baby dragon," says Beau.

I bury my smile in Jade's fur. "Brother Beau." I like saying that.

"Ox and Monkey, good bond. Very strong."

"Ox? You're an Ox?"

"Ox, patient. Good fellow. Needs smart Monkey."

Beau extends his hand. My palm and fingers curl around his.

"Sister Sugar." I like hearing that.

"Brother Beau."

ॐ

Come evening, I study the stars. Billy taught me to see Orion and Pegasus, the flying horse. I search for rabbits, cats, and monkeys.

Kerosene lamps flicker. Fireflies dodge among tree limbs. The air is moist, hot. Everyone lingers outside. No one wants to go inside, sleep, even though we know there's work tomorrow.

"Sister Sugar, gift."

Beau hands me a roll of soft paper. I uncurl it on the porch. Black ink has made shapes. Outlines of places. Swirls of water. Mountain peaks.

I point. "China." I remember the shapes Beau drew in the dirt. "America.

"Thank you, Beau."

He points to the bottom corner:

I've seen this picture before. "My name?"

Beau hands me a quill. Feathers on one end; sharp point on the other. He opens a case, spits, then mixes it with a stick. "Sugar," he says. "Sugar." He's encouraging me again.

I think Beau must really be my brother. He knows exactly what I need.

I dip the quill in the black paste, especially where it's soft and runny.

On the map, I write:

"Mercy, Sugar, did Beau teach you that?" asks Mister Beale. "Come see. Everyone, come see. Sugar can write."

River Road folks are peering over my shoulder, staring at my marks.

"That's my name." Not drawn perfect. Not as pretty as Beau's.

Restless, my stomach turns. I lean closer, studying the boundaries. Voices—Chinese and African—fade. Mouths move, but I can't hear words. Just my own heart. I think I hear Beau's heart, too. And Jade's heartbeat, racing happily, happily next to me.

Amazing. A map of the world.

I whisper into Beau's ear, "Where can I go, Beau?"

"Anywhere."

Almost Done

We're all working. Beau's in front of me and Mister Beale behind me. We're moving as one. *Cut-cut-cutting cane.* Bodies just move. Not much time to think. No play. Or sleep. Another season is coming to an end.

Billy, our Overseer, runs everywhere, making sure the cane gets cut, the line stays in rhythm and together. His pa is proud.

Manon and Annie feed us. They work hard over the community fire, making gumbo, red beans, and rice. Annie even tried to make dumplings. They weren't very good, but everybody ate them anyway.

I've made a new work song:

> *Cut-cut-China. Cut-cut-ocean.*
> *Cut-cut-America. Louisiana, too.*
> *Cut-cut-north. Cut-cut-south.*
> *If sugar can sail, I can, too.*

Whack. The cane is cut, starts to fall. *Whack.* I pull it loose, lay it on a stack.

Flies, bees. Too much sun. I pull my hat lower, wrap cotton around my face, leaving only my eyes to see.

Mister Beale drags and throws cane into the hand-push wagon. Master Liu and Mister Petey bend, push up and down on the metal rod, making the wagon inch down the rails to the sugar mill. Up, down, up, down, over and over. Just like *whack-whack-whack* over and over.

Sunrise to sundown. Lamps and campfires bloom all night. Everyone works, weaving, swaying. Until their eyes droop into sleep.

Mister Beale tries to catch folks before they hit the ground. Machetes are sharp.

Hay mattresses are on the big house porch. An hour of sleep, no more!

We all work hard. Before rains come. Before frost. Before cane starts rotting and the sugar inside it turns bitter.

In the mill house, Mister Waters boils syrup. Mister Zheng feeds the fire. Missus Celeste rakes the sugar to dry, then separates brown and white crystals. White sugar brings more money. Once we finish cutting, the mill will keep busy. Tons of sugar will have to be packed into sacks for shipping.

My knees ache, my back hurts; my hands are cut; my face, scratched.

"Push," hollers Mister Beale. "We're almost done."
Cut, snap, crack that cane.

Like magic, the Chinese unleash their energy and race ahead. *Whack. Cut. Cut. Cut.* I marvel at how beautiful they look. Twisting bodies, swinging arms. Every one of them is so fast, so strong.

River Road folks are beautiful, too. Age slows them. But they, too, are giving all they can.

Me and Billy grunt. *Whack.*

I can't sing. I can't speak. *Whack-whack-whack.*

I hate, hate, hate sugar! Then I grin. *Whack!*

My friend Billy works beside me. Sugar brought the Chinese men. Brought Beau.

It's getting harder to hate sugar.

Dawn. We've worked through the night.

"Last row, last row," shouts Mister Beale.

Everybody roars, *whacking.* Chinese, River Road folks, Mister Wills, Billy—everybody is hacking the very last row!

The cane falls like sad sticks, tumbling, tumbling down.

*   *   *

"Best Overseer I ever had!" Mister Wills pats Billy's back.

Billy hugs his pa. Weary, even us workers grin.

Harvest is done.

Happy?

Billy!" I scream at the big house. "We're cele-brating. We're going to have a bonfire. You've got to come. We'll have dragon, Br'er Rabbit tales."

"I'm coming, Sugar," shouts Billy, coming out the door and leaping off the porch.

"Billy Wills, you come back here."

"Aw, Ma."

Missus Wills is on the porch. "Wait. Can't go visit-ing without taking food. Manon and Annie fixed a basket."

Billy doesn't want to wait, but I don't mind waiting for food.

"Go on, Billy," Mister Wills shouts from the upstairs window. "We'll have Manon bring the basket."

Me and Billy start running.

"Sugar!"

I halt. "Mister Wills, I didn't do nothin' wrong!"

"Me, either," says Billy, though his name wasn't even hollered!

"Be good, Sugar. No trouble."

We run like lightning. Moonlight guides our path.

"Let's make a ruckus," says Billy.

I don't answer. I just run harder. I'm going to beat Billy Wills.

ॐ

The fields of cane are all cut. Hacked-down stalks stretch into the distance.

We've worked hard the whole season. Spring. Summer. Fall.

Tonight, Mister Waters will let the cauldron cool.

Missus Celeste will stop sorting crystals. We'll all celebrate. A special extra night of rest—Billy convinced his pa. Afterward, the final cooking, boxing of sugar to ship to the world.

I'm already planning off-season. I'll practice writing, Chinese and English. Make new games with Billy. Raft. I'm going to learn to say "My name is Sugar" in Chinese.

৵৹

Bellies stuffed, me and Billy sit on my shack steps. The bonfire, six feet high, burns beautiful, like a nighttime sun.

Master Liu, Mister Chin, and Beau have made Chinese lanterns. Sticks and paper boxes of color that glow red and yellow. Gold threads dangle from their four corners.

Mister Zheng smokes a pipe with Mister Beale. Missus Wills hands potato pie to Master Liu. Missus Thornton passes sugar squares. All the Chinese take one.

Missus Thornton puckers her mouth; she offers me a square. I take one, too. Missus Thornton smiles like she's gone to heaven.

I bite. I don't like it. Sickly sweet. "Thank you, Missus Thornton," I say, hiding the remains in my shawl.

Billy takes two and stuffs his mouth. "Mmmm. Good."

"Sister Sugar. Billy."

Beau doesn't shout, but I can tell his voice anywhere. It cuts through the *pop-crackle* of the fire, folks chattering. He's hiding something behind his back.

"I have a present. For both of you."

"It's like Christmas," says Billy.

"Both of you must make it work."

"Work? I'm tired of work."

"Different kind of work, Sugar. See. Dragon's head." *Whoosh*. He pulls out a yellow dragonhead with big eyes, a red tongue, and pointed ears. "His tail." *Whoosh*. Beau lifts high a flowing yellow tail. It's like a kite's tail, but longer, with flaps that flutter.

"In China, we celebrate dragon. We cover ourselves, like this"—Beau swoops the dragon head over his face—"and use side sticks to shake and bend the dragon's head."

Beau starts stomping around the yard. Firelight makes the dragon's head glow. River Road folks are awestruck. "Beautiful." "Wonderful."

Beau is a yellow big-headed, big-eyed, big-mouthed dragon.

"Let me, let me," I plead.

Beau laughs. "Who will be the head? And who will be the tail?"

"I'm the head," says Billy.

"No, me."

"Take turns," says Beau.

Billy grabs the head and I scowl. I hold the two sticks and pull the long tail over my head and back.

"Shake, Sugar."

I shake. The tail wiggles and flows, and the flaps flutter and slap.

Billy moves first, his dragon's head bobbing. I skip to keep up so it won't look like the dragon's tail fell off! Billy starts stomping—*bam-bam-bam*. I stomp,

too. Soon our dragon is moving fierce. *Bam-bam-bam.*
The head is swaying side to side, up and down; the
tail is flopping low and high, spinning all around.

River Road folks clap, shout with joy.

Me and Billy make the best dragon.

ॐ

"My turn to tell story," says Beau. "Another tale of
how Dragon helped Emperor."

"Emperor Jade?" I ask. "Where's Jade? Jade wants
to hear the story, too. Jade," I start calling. But Jade
is nowhere!

"We'll wait, Sugar," says Beau. "Jade can't be far."

"I'll help," says Billy. "I'll check near the house,
Sugar. You check near the mill."

I'm off, running, calling, "Jade. Jade."

Jade has become family, too. When he's near, I
feel calm.

"Jade." I look beneath bushes, up in trees. Jade isn't
at the well. Isn't in the garden. Isn't on the path.

I still hear River Road folks happy, having a good

time. Mister Wills's voice booms; Master Liu is chirping high. Mister Beale chuckles, a deep bass.

I keep running toward the mill, hollering, "Jade. Come hear about the Emperor. Dragons."

It's a full moon. My shadow runs beside me. My legs are strong; my shift flares. I run across shadows of bare branches, bushes, and stones.

Smoke irritates my nose.

Something makes me stop, spin around. I feel haunted, like some doom is following me. I can't hear any people. Only rustling. Maybe birds settling in trees? Branches snapping. Maybe a rabbit settling to ground? I hear shrieks. Some animal—mouse?—trying to escape. From what? An owl.

I keep running. "Jade! Come out."

Dark and darker shadows. There are no lamps, no campfire or bonfire. No candles. Only moonlight, wind, quivering branches and leaves.

I'm all alone. Nobody's moving but me.

I'm starting to feel scared.

*   *   *

Ahead, the mill looms, even bigger than the plantation house. Black wood, black metal roof with chimney spouts for escaping steam and sugar smoke.

I see light.

The mill's supposed to be dark.

The light sways. Someone's inside, carrying a light.

"Who's there?" I shout.

The mill window goes dark. It must've been a lamp. Not a candle. A kerosene lamp glows bright.

Someone's in the mill when they aren't supposed to be.

They don't want to be seen. This worries me. I don't want to be blamed for other people's trouble.

I start tiptoeing backward.

Meow.

I can't help but coo, "Jade? Here, Jade. Here, kitty, kitty."

More meows. Screeching, lamenting like Billy's violin. Jade sounds as scared as I feel.

The lamp flickers again, floating low then high. High, higher. The lamp crashes down. Flames shoot up.

I gasp.

Fire.

Jade! I start running toward the huge mill doors.

A door slams open. Mister Tom pushes past me.

"What'd you do? What'd you do?" I yell.

Mister Tom snarls, "Get out of my way." His face is pale, his hair slicked black. He raises his hand; I duck.

Jade cries, pitiful.

"No sugar's leaving here. Tell Wills I done it. I don't care. Blacks should keep their place."

Mister Tom looks awful. Angry, scared. Hurt. Evil, like the devil, all mixed up. "Not sorry," he says, disappearing into the night shadows.

Beyond the mill doors, flames are licking high. Red, yellow, blue. Kerosene has spilled on the floor; flames are spreading, lighting the kindling and branches beneath the three kettles, and burning empty and filled canvas bags of sugar.

Jade yowls, but I can't see him.

"*Sugar!*" Billy's running, cutting across the grass.

"Fire, Billy. Ring the bell. Ring the bell!"

Billy halts, shouts, "What about you?"

"Jade's inside. I've got to help him."

"No, Sugar! No!"

Smoke rolls out the door in thick waves.

"Ring the bell," I scream. "Get help." Inhaling, I pinch my nose and duck inside. The heat stuns me. Fire sounds like thunder. Except it doesn't fade—it grows louder and louder. Flames lick the walls, the empty cauldron. Cane, stacked along the walls, curls and burns. Sacks of sugar melt. The cauldron's fire is lit, burning ghostly blue-red.

I exhale. My next breath hurts. Smoke burns my nose and throat. Heat sears my insides. I drop to my knees, coughing.

"Jade," I gasp. "Jade." A shadow, near the window, inches forward.

"Jade. Come on."

Another inch. Moonlight captures his face. Green eyes wide, head and ears pulled back, he stretches out a singed paw.

"Jade, please. Come."

He doesn't move. Eyes shutting, he rolls, collapses onto his side.

I drop to my knees and crawl. Cinders burn. I'm moving nearer and nearer the flames. Flames, jagged red, race to meet me. I start to cry; I've got to save him.

"Jade!" My eyes sting, but I keep focused, keep crawling, even though a voice inside me says, "Turn and run."

I lift Jade, holding him close. His fur is burnt, patches of skin blistering.

"Sugar!" Billy's in the doorway.

"Run," I try to shout, but smoke chokes my throat. "Run," I scream, words stuck in my head.

Melted sugar spreads, runs like water. Syrup bubbles over, dripping from the cauldron. It swirls closer.

Billy picks a path toward me and Jade.

"No," I try to yell, but cough.

A beam falls. An explosion of smoke, sparks, and flame. "Bil...ly" rips from me. Coughing, croaking, trying to call his name again, I keep watch for Billy.

Flames tower everywhere. Timbers burn. Sugar

smells sweet and scorched. The roof cracks open. Holes of smoke and starlight. All that's left of the mill is hellfire heat, stabbing smoke, and a red-hot cauldron.

Holding Jade, chin on my chest, I cry. Billy's gone. Me and the cat are going to burn.

"Sugar. Sugar." The call is muffled. Overhead. Another explosion. Glass shards fall. *Whooshing* fire sucks through the broken window. I scream. Syrup burns my shoes and feet.

"Come on, Sugar. Give me your hand."

A miracle. Billy's no longer inside but outside. His hand reaches through the broken window.

"Billy, take him." Standing on tiptoe, I push Jade, limp, up and through the window.

"Now you," says Billy. My head bleeds. Dizzy, I can't stand, climb the wall. Behind me, it's hotter and hotter. Flames and scalding syrup will kill me.

"Come on, Sugar. Please."

I jump, reaching for Billy's hand.

Bad Dreams

S ugar."
The cane field calls, like a bogeyman trying to scare me.

"*Sugarrrr. Sugarrr.*"

I won't listen. I twist, and pain shoots up my leg.
In the distance, a bird tweets.

"*Sugarrrrrrrrr.*"

I'm startled awake. My leg and feet are wrapped in
bandages. Honey salve soaks my fingers. I hurt, a
burning, stinging hurt. Then, I remember the mill.
Jade. My heart is heavy like a rock.

I close my eyes.

My heart feels like it's being squeezed. I open my eyes. Jade is sitting on my chest, his green eyes looking at me. His paws press, move up and down on me, like sticks on a drum. Patches of his fur are gone. He's ugly but beautiful at the same time.

Jade purrs.

I scratch his head.

Tail flicking, he lies beside me. Wincing, I shift my body to my good side and lay my hand on his white tummy. He doesn't move. I sigh.

Someone has rekindled the fire. There's a glass of water on the floor. Corn bread on a plate.

My legs hurt bad; Jade's skin must, too. There's a blanket over me, a fat pillow beneath my head.

Jade's tummy goes in and out, his chest rises and falls. I feel the beat of his heart.

A bird tweets again. No, it's whistling. "Billy? Billy?"

The door opens. Billy pokes his head in. His grin makes my heart race.

"You whistle good," I say.

"I know. I've been waiting for you to wake up."

"Sitting on the porch?"

"Whistling my heart out. You scared me."

"I scared me, too."

Billy lifts Jade.

And I remember. *Billy saving me, pulling me through the window, smoke and flames shooting, rolling behind me.*

The sugar mill explodes, the roof shifts, falls, showering sparks.

"You didn't ring the bell?"

"No. There wasn't time. Everyone heard the explosions."

"I remember." *Worried voices asking, "She all right?" Mister Beale lifting me. Me whimpering, "Jade?" Hearing Beau's voice, say, "I've got him, Sugar."*

Nothing more. Only quiet, darkness.

"You've been sleeping. 'Healing,' says Master Liu. Worse than my brain fever." Billy sits on the edge of my hay mattress.

"You brought me the pillow and blanket?"

"Told Ma it wasn't fair. You needed comfort."

"Thank you, Billy." I'm weary, sore.

"I've been here every day. Told Ma and Pa both they couldn't stop me."

I'm listening hard to Billy's words. Trying to hear what he isn't saying.

"Everybody else?"

"Trying to salvage what little wood, sugar there is."

My eyes start to close.

"Pa thought you did it."

"No."

"I told him it was Tom. I saw him."

"Did you?"

"I did, Sugar. And even if I didn't, I'd never believe you'd hurt anyone or anything."

I blink, gulp tears.

"Want some water, Sugar?"

My throat's sore. But I'm thirstier than I've ever been. I sip while Billy holds the cup.

"Jade hasn't left your side."

I feel grateful. I saved him. And Billy saved me.

"Thank you, Billy." But my words don't seem meaningful enough. Pain rises in my body; my mind tells me to sleep.

"Lots of change, Sugar."

I open my eyes. Billy's gotten older. He's serious, his face and arms suntanned and strong.

"Pa's hurt 'cause a white man burnt his mill. Ruined everything. He thought he knew Mister Tom. He thought he knew me. He's still trying to understand you're the best friend I've ever had. 'The world is upside down,' he says."

I swallow; my throat's thick.

I hear a twinkling sound. Billy isn't whistling. I feel I'm floating free.

"Ma?" I murmur.

"Go to sleep, Sugar," answers Billy. "We aren't going anywhere."

※

Jade and Monkey ride on Ox's back. Ox clip-clops up a gangplank. On the steamer, there's no sugar. Just animals. Br'er Rabbit. Horse. Hyena. Rooster. Even Turtle.

"Ahoy," *shouts Ox.*

"Ahoy," *shouts Monkey.*

The ship's paddle starts churning, splashing, spraying water.

⊰͡

I wake. Feeling alert, excited. Feeling as if my stinging, hurtful burns are reminding me I'm alive. "Billy?"

"I'm here."

"Help me go outside." I want to see the sky, dirt, and water.

Billy helps me stand; I lean on him, walking slow. "I had the best dream, Billy. Off on an adventure."

"I like that, Sugar."

Outside, the light is bright. I squint. Smoke still rises everywhere. The fields burn too sweet, turning cane to ash. The smoldering mill smells bitter.

I sway on the porch rocker. Billy squats beside me. "Is Mister Tom in jail?"

Billy shakes his head. "No. There's lots who think like Mister Tom. Pa's hurt. Doesn't understand why the sheriff says there's been no crime. Why some folks—white folks—want to see Pa fail."

"I'm sorry, Billy."

And I am. Even though I don't like Mister Wills much, Billy does. Billy's my friend, and he loves his pa.

My body hurts but not as much as my heart.

Changes

I'm almost healed. Jade hasn't left my side. Beau
and Mister Beale tell me stories, a different tale
every day. Missus Beale cooks her best food.
Billy keeps me company, even when I'm grumpy
because I can't run and play. Evenings, Master Liu
sits quietly beside me on the porch as Mister Zheng
lets me win at checkers.

I have scars on my legs, but I hurt less and less.

Grown folks are upset. Off-season should be joyful.
But the burnt mill, the burnt sugar crop makes
everyone sad. All our work has disappeared.

Through the wall, I hear the Beales talking late into the night. "Lost crop, lost money." I don't understand. Mister Wills has paid us already.

Worry floats inside the Beales' words.

⅋

"Look." From the porch, I see Mister Wills walking toward the shacks.

Mister Beale and Master Liu both stand. Billy sets down his harmonica.

I can't help but be nervous. Mister Wills in our yard never means any good. I can see he's nervous, too.

"Everybody, outside. I have something to say." His voice is dry, strained.

Standing, his back round, his stomach jutting, he looks woeful and tired.

Folks gather. Mister Petey must've been shaving; half his face is soapy. Missus Ellie looks disheveled, like she's woken from a nap. Others head toward our porch to hear Mister Wills.

Mister Wills wipes his brow. He doesn't speak.

I lean forward. Usually Mister Wills just says his mind. Folks shift, shuffle, wringing their heads and hands.

"I've sold River Road."

I didn't know you could sell a whole world.

Folks look at one another, disbelieving. Mister Beale grips the porch rail. Master Liu is tense, wary.

"No sugar to sell. I don't have money to plant next year's crop. Sold River Road to Jean DeLavier."

Someone else will own River Road? Where will Billy live? Where will we?

"DeLavier's been wanting my land. Wanting to expand his fields."

Billy runs to his pa's side.

Loss is etched on Mister Wills's face. Billy's bewildered. I'm just confused.

What will happen to me, to the Beales, Beau, and Billy?

Mister Beale grips the rail so tight, I think he's going to break it. Master Liu walks into the yard to calm his people.

"You've all been good workers," says Mister Wills, surveying, staring at each one of us. He nods at me. For the first time, I think he truly sees me.

"You're free to stay or go." His words are like a thunderclap. Missus Beale bites her lip. Reverend Thornton bows his head.

I clasp Beau's hand. River Road is gone.

"Me, Missus Wills, and Billy will be leaving for New Orleans next week."

"No," I holler, leaping up. Pain shoots through my legs. Beau steadies me, keeps me from falling over.

Billy runs back to me. "I don't want to go, Sugar." His face is all bunched up.

He won't cry. I won't, either.

"You're leaving," I murmur. "Like Lizzie did."

"Billy!" says Mister Wills.

He looks back at his pa. He looks at me. "It isn't fair." He goes to join his pa.

I collapse into the rocker.

"Can't say we didn't see this coming," Missus Beale says to Mister Beale.

I didn't see it coming. Billy and his pa head for the big house.

"We've survived worse," answers Mister Beale. He looks out into the yard. "We've survived worse," he repeats again, loudly. "We're still free. We still do good work."

Black and Chinese folks nod.

"Mister Beale, wise," says Master Liu. "We do good work." Then he speaks Chinese, walks toward his shack, and the other Chinese follow.

"We've survived worse," says Mister Petey. "Hard work is what owners understand."

"Hard work," repeats Mister Beale. "Keep doing our work, we'll be all right."

I'm tired of working just to be all right.

Jade leaps onto my lap. I squeeze him too tight, and he struggles. "Sorry, Jade."

I look at the Beales, the other ex-slaves, slowly heading toward their shacks.

We got freedom, but the Beales, me, everyone else are stuck at River Road.

"Do. See. Feel."

Jade's green eyes widen, glittering with yellow specks. I think he hears my thoughts bellowing inside me.

Ma wouldn't want me to stay put now. I can't wait for Pa anymore.

For the first time, I feel certain Pa is dead. It's been eleven years. If he could've come back, he'd already be here.

I realize I must leave River Road.

The Wave

The air is crisp. I'm wrapped tightly in my shawl, watching the sun glowing on the horizon. It's bittersweet, seeing the miles of cleared fields. Cane will grow again, but it'll be different. My hands won't cut it.

Smoke rises from the shacks' chimneys. Rooster Ugly crows.

A flock of blackbirds streak past clouds, the purple-red sky. I feel different, restless, in a new way.

*　　*　　*

The Willses are leaving. Their furniture is going to be shipped on a barge. Mister Wills sits atop the wagon; Missus Wills, wearing a yellow bonnet, is at his side. Manon and Annie sit in the wagon bed, their legs dangling off the edge. Billy holds the brown mare's reins. We've all come to say good-bye.

Me and Beau made a dragon kite. "Here, Billy. Beau drew the face. I dyed the streamers for his tail."

"It's beautiful. Thank you, Sugar. Thank Beau, too."

"I will." Grown folks are leaving us alone. "I'm happy for you, Billy. You always wanted to leave River Road."

"Not like this."

I pat the mare. "Times are surely changing, Billy Wills."

Billy's grown taller than me. "Shake." Billy's hands are rough like mine. I hold on, not letting go. "I won't forget you, Billy."

"I won't forget you, Sugar." His voice trembles, chokes. He places his foot in the stirrup, clutches the saddle horn, and lifts himself up and over. The mare sidesteps. I pull back.

"Pa, I'm ready."

"Let's go, then."

Billy looks down. "Bye, Sugar." He taps the mare with his heels. He follows behind the wagon. He won't look back. I just know it.

ॐ

Me and Beau toss grain, feeding the chicks.

"Here, Peanut. Here." A chicken juts its head. I think it's Peanut, but it's hard to tell. All the chicks have grown. I shoo Rooster Ugly.

"Sister Sugar, let's sit."

"For a story?"

"No." Beau squats. His face is level with mine. He looks more serious than I've ever seen him.

"You're leaving," I say.

He doesn't answer, and that's how I know it's true. "I want to go, too."

Beau hugs me. I feel steady, safe. He gently pushes me back. "What about the Beales?"

I sigh, heavy.

"They're old."

"You're right, Beau. They need me. But I want to leave, Beau. They want to stay."

"You, fix."

I don't know how to fix, I think. My stomach churns. "What if I need to find you?"

"You have map."

I do—a map of the whole world. "Where will you be, Beau?"

"Hawaii. An island. Waipahu Plantation."

I nod.

Beau's eyes sparkle. "Me and Master Liu be there."

≈

All day, I listen to grown folks talk. Mister Zheng is staying on the plantation. Him and Mister Waters both. They'll cut cane and play checkers.

Missus Celeste is staying. "All I know is how to separate sugar."

Reverend tells everyone, "River Road was where I was called to preach. As a young slave, cutting cane, I felt God's grace. My place is here." Missus Thornton beams like she's happy. Quiet Mister Aires says, "I'll stay. But not if DeLavier cuts my pay."

Missus Ellie weeps. "This is where I want to be buried."

Beau and Master Liu don't say anything. I think their leaving must be a secret. Not a bad secret, just something they're keeping private. Beau told me because I'm family. The Beales are my family, too.

All day, the Beales do chores. They don't say nothin'. It drives me crazy.

But Missus Beale sews, boils laundry in a pot, hangs it on a rope tied between trees. Mister Beale saws, stacks wood, fills the oil lamps, and patches his leather shoe.

Work, work, work. Acting like nothing's changed.

Missus Beale looks like she hasn't slept. Dark shadows her eyes. Mister Beale's jaw stays clenched. He's so sad-eyed, he looks like he'll never tell a story again.

Inside my shack, I decide to surprise the Beales. I

start making supper. I boil black-eyed peas, add a ham bone and hot peppers. I cry slicing onions.

I mix egg, cornmeal, and water into cakes. I use a spatula to shape them into circles. I flip them when their sides turn brown.

I go to the well and fill a pitcher with water.

"Supper," I yell. "Mister and Missus Beale, I made supper. Come eat."

Missus Beale is still hanging sheets. I clasp her hand, pulling her inside my shack.

"There's work to do."

"Missus Beale, work's done for the day."

Mister Beale, in the doorway, rubs his hands. "I'm hungry. What've you made, Sugar?"

"Wait, Mister Beale. We've got to get Missus Beale comfortable."

"Humph."

I lay my shawl on the floor. "Sit here." I hand her a cup of water.

"I should be taking care of you."

"You always take care of me." I smile innocently.

"You're up to something, Sugar."

"No, I'm not. You fed me when I was sick, my turn to feed you."

"Smells good," says Mister Beale, sitting cross-legged on the floor.

Missus Beale squints. "I think I should heat up some greens in the pan."

"Nope. I made peas and cakes." I fill a bowl for each, lay the cakes on a plate. All three of us sit and eat.

"Mighty fine," says Mister Beale. "Thank you, Sugar."

"You're a good cook," says Missus Beale. "Like my daughter." Mourning flashes inside her eyes.

Mister Beale pats her hand. "It's all right, Eugenie."

But it's not all right, I think. Year after year of cutting cane 'til I grow old. Years of working for an owner in the big house, long after the Beales have passed. I want more. I want to do something else, see the world, and be free of sugar.

"We're going north," I blurt.

"Can't do that, Sugar."

"Yes, we can. I'm taking you. Time for you to find your children."

"We wouldn't know where to start."

"We'll start in St. Louis. That's where Lizzie went."

Both look at me, skeptical. Like I'm making up a nonsense tale.

I almost stop. "I mean it. We're leaving."

"We're too old. Too slow," says Missus Beale.

"You are old. Too old to stay here. River Road isn't going to be River Road anymore."

"Sugar, you're too young to understand."

"I am not."

"Well, we're not leaving," says Mister Beale sharply.

"You're both acting like Hyena."

"Sugar, apologize."

"I won't, Missus Beale. Hyena wouldn't leave if his village caught fire. But Br'er Rabbit would tell everybody, 'Go.' Turtle, Tiger, and all the animals would leave. Find another home." I'm breathing hard. "Please, Mister and Missus Beale. Let's go. There's nothing here."

Mister Beale says, "The bad I know..."

"...is better than what I don't," finishes Missus Beale.

The Beales are in my shack. Sitting on the dirt. There's no table. No bed off the ground. Nothing but a bed sack, a fireplace, and cooking gear. No window to let in light. How can any place not be better than here?

Mister Beale looks wistful. I know they want to leave, find their children. But they're scared to try.

Propped against the wall is my map. "Look, Mister Beale, the world is big, but we've got a map."

I unroll the map on the floor.

"Here's us. And here's St. Louis. We just have to stay on the river."

I flatten my hand on the map. "See, St. Louis is hardly farther than my fingertips. It's closer than the size of your hand, Mister Beale."

"We don't have the energy, Sugar," says Missus Beale. "If we were younger..."

"But it can't be harder than cutting cane next year. Year after year. Sunup to sundown."

Then I ask, "Which sounds better: cutting cane or finding your children?"

The Beales look at each other.

"You know I won't stop pestering you until you say yes."

Missus Beale nods to Mister Beale.

Mister Beale says, "You win, Sugar. I guess it would be better to head north...."

I twirl. "Promise?"

"Promise."

I dash straight for the Beales. We hug, good and tight.

I run outside, shout from the porch, "Me and the Beales are going north."

Neighbors hoot, whistle, and clap. This time, it will be everyone else that has to be happy for us.

Across the yard, Beau bows to me. I bow back.

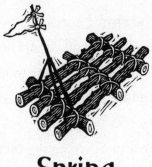

Spring

M e and the Beales are on a steamship heading north to St. Louis. We left River Road three days ago. The river is so much bigger than I imagined.

Jade's with us, too, chasing rats in the ship's hold.

Leaning on the rail, I watch rippling white waves caused by the churning paddle wheel. Spray settles on my face and arms. I inhale, smelling mud and fish. Dogwoods and magnolias line the shore. On my map, the Mississippi reaches far, far past St. Louis. One day, I'll travel to its northern end.

I like how the river's horizon touches sky. I like how blue-green algae floats, sparkling in the sunshine. I like the unsteadiness of water beneath the ship. I like standing still while the ship carries me farther than I've ever been.

I think of me and Billy playing pirates. Both captains on our raft. I think about how he knew I didn't like my name. So long ago and far away now.

Here, on the river, I realize I like my name. Ma gave it to me. I wrap my arms about myself and imagine her hugging me.

I'm free.

A Note from the Author

In 2007, my friend Edwardo e-mailed me a review of Lucy M. Cohen's book *Chinese in the Post–Civil War South: A People Without a History*. Ed knew I'd been traveling to Chengdu, China, to teach creative writing. He also knew I'd be captivated by an American history I hadn't known.

I kept daydreaming about Chinese and African Americans in Louisiana, working side by side. I could hear the cadence of their voices... see them cooking, resting after a hard day in the fields.

For a long time, I thought I'd write an adult novel.

But, in 2010, I visualized a little girl, hands on her hips, who kept complaining, "How come I have to work? How come I can't play?"

Sugar was born. She became the heroine who bridged cultures and encouraged joy.

Reconstruction in America was a turbulent time. Some Southerners wanted slavery to continue; others adapted to a free labor source. Labor shortages were common, as many African Americans migrated north and to other parts of the United States.

Thousands of Chinese workers were brought from China, the Caribbean, Latin America, and British Guiana (Guyana) to Mississippi and Louisiana to work on sugarcane plantations. These workers, while immigrants and, some, indentured servants, were at times treated as brutally as slaves. American politicians passed specific laws that prevented Chinese immigrants from gaining citizenship. Some went on to the Hawaiian Islands, gaining land and starting businesses and new lives.

River Road Plantation is modeled after Laura Plantation in Louisiana. Alcée Fortier, professor of romance languages at Tulane University, collected *Compair Lapin* tales (Br'er Rabbit, "Brother Rabbit" variations of West African folktales) at Laura Plantation and elsewhere.

In 1894, Fortier published *Louisiana Folk-Tales: In French Dialect and English Translation*. Some Br'er Rabbit tales originally did involve hyenas, a common African animal, and later were translated into foxes for American audiences. Br'er Rabbit was a trickster—a heroic, wily figure for slaves because he outwitted the hyena/fox, which was symbolic of white slave owners. Even Br'er Rabbit's laziness was a triumph in a world where slaves were inhumanely treated and harshly worked. Br'er Rabbit tales were entertaining and inspiring, and an act of hidden defiance for slaves. They also contributed to slaves' and freed people's sense of community, honoring the *griot*, the storyteller tradition of Africa. (Famed author Joel Chandler Harris is rightfully recognized for translating and retelling oral Br'er Rabbit stories for the American literary canon.)

Dragon tales, like Br'er Rabbit tales, are equally inspiring to the Chinese. Dragons are spiritual figures who promote peace, justice, and plenty.

The Chinese calendar is built around twelve animals—including the Hare. Hare was Americanized to Rabbit.

It is true that people born in the Year of the Monkey and the Year of the Ox make strong bonds. It is also true that according to southern folklore, turtles bring good luck.

Beau and Sugar create what is a uniquely (and increasingly) American family—namely, a family that blends multiethnic bloodlines. Billy is a hero, too. He represents all the southern Reconstructionist youths who grew up in the shadow of slavery but learned to form friendships based upon character, not skin color. Billy, Beau, and Sugar represent the best of America.

Sincerely,
Jewell

Acknowledgments

Books are collaborations. I wish to thank my husband, Brad, for his loving support; my editor, Liza Baker, who guided me with brilliant grace; her assistant, Allison Moore, who brought such cheer to the process; and the many Little, Brown Books for Young Readers employees who took such great care of *Sugar*.

Special thanks, also, to my research assistant, Catherine Murray, and to Dr. Robert J. Cutter, professor of Chinese, director of the School for International Letters and Cultures at Arizona State University.

Also by Jewell Parker Rhodes:

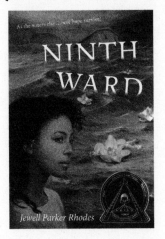

As the waters rise . . . will hope survive?

NINTH
WARD

Jewell Parker Rhodes

Twelve-year-old Lanesha lives in a tight-knit community in New Orleans's Ninth Ward. She doesn't have a fancy house, like her uptown family, or lots of friends, like the other kids on her street. But she does have Mama Ya-Ya, her fiercely loving caretaker, wise in the ways of the world and able to predict the future. So when Mama Ya-Ya's visions show a powerful hurricane—Katrina—fast approaching, it's up to Lanesha to call upon the hope and strength Mama Ya-Ya has given her to help them both survive the storm.

Ninth Ward is a deeply emotional story about transformation and a celebration of resilience, friendship, and family—as only love can define it.

Available now